View From My Rear Window

View From My Rear Window

ISBN: 9781532383670

Book Cover by: Walter Brinkley

For other books by E.L. Rhodes visit *www.elrhodesbooks.com*

For My V.R.R.'s

View From My Rear Window

The story you are about to read is almost true... The names have been changed to protect the ignorant.

Introduction

The loud successions of buzzing still echo throughout the entire cell block as I lie here quietly on my cot staring at the ceiling as the doors slam loudly shut. Staring aimlessly, reflecting and revisiting the events that led to my internment. It's been three long years. Three long years since I've had a good meal or felt the soft touch of a woman, my woman, Michelle. Though it was the love for this woman that has placed me here. Here in this dark, lonely cell and yet, I still miss her. How her enchanting powers and my love for her led to murder still bewilders me. How did she control me like that I continue to wonder? It seems that my lustful quest for sex finally contributed toward getting the better of me but it was not sex alone. If we were talking about any other woman I'd probably agree with you but not Michelle, with her it was love. Even at this very moment I still feel like her fool, a slave for her. One that would do anything for her, even kill.

This is how I now spend my days, thinking about Michelle and the killing. You see, this wasn't your ordinary everyday kill forged from the heat of passion, a jealous rage, self-defense or a kill for someone's riches. No, the sole origin of this killing, was love. A killing that had been planted and nurtured over time and time, is what I got. How did I get here?

Let's start from the beginning.

Chapter 1 - The Appointment

I can still remember how the warm splashes splattered up the back of my bright white tee shirt as I pedaled faster than ever down the wet pavement. It had rained earlier and I had pestered my mother to no end to let me go out shortly after the rain had subsided. As soon as the sun reappeared, off I went. I loved the outdoors, it was my refuge. And those wonderful days still remain clear inside my head as if it was just yesterday. I lie here reminiscing about the golden days of childhood, laughter, and love. For it was then that I had discovered my first true love. It was with her that I found my first kiss, my first friend, and ultimately, my first heartbreak.

I had just been promoted to the sixth grade and she to the seventh when the first appointment was scheduled; that's what we called them then. She lived alone with her mother just up the block from me. Her name was Michelle, Michelle Taylor and from the very first moment that I laid eyes on her, I adored her. Yep, it was love at first sight. I loved everything about her in that split second. She was a sweet, light complexioned girl with dark frizzy hair and was what we referred to as "high yellow" back then. I'm not sure if her dad was white or maybe just very light in complexion himself but Michelle, she was as close to white as they came. Her hair was shoulder length and her lips were full and as red as pomegranates. She had large dark eyes that you could easily get lost in. And through my eyes, she was the most beautiful girl ever.

The morning of our first scheduled appointment, I walked up to the door and rang the bell shortly after her mother had driven off for work. It was summer, the year, 1969. It was late June and we were out from school. Although she was only twelve, her mother felt comfortable with leaving her alone while she worked. Let's face it, times were different then. People still slept with their front doors open, didn't lock their car doors, and looked out for one another.

I stood anxiously wondering if I should ring the bell a second time before the sound of approaching footsteps caught my attention. The door slowly opened and I was quickly greeted by the receptionist, Allison. At only twelve years old, Allison was already five feet eight inches tall and towered over me. She looked over her eyeglasses down at me before she smiled and greeted me, "Yes sir, may I help you?" I smiled back at her before responding, "Yes, I'm here for my nine o'clock appointment."

"Why yes sir, come right in. Miss Taylor can see you now," she responded.

Allison was Michelle's best friend and her next-door neighbor who was always present whenever anyone saw Michelle. She was always around even when I preferred her not to be. I would constantly be reminded of how close I couldn't get to Michelle just by Allison's protective glares alone most days.

After Allison had pushed the door open wide enough for me to enter, I walked inside and gazed at my beauty as she sat comfortably on the long sofa. Michelle turned and looked at me before producing that smile that would somehow seem to swallow me up and devour me. I paused for just a moment before gathering myself then walked around to the front of her resting place and sat down next to her. I had barely lowered myself into the seat before my heart began pounding like a Zulu drum. It performed in this way every time I was in her presence. I placed my arm around her shoulders like I had seen in so many movies then quickly licked the dryness from my lips in preparation for my servicing. She looked over at Allison and asked her for the time.

"It's 9:13," Allison said still playing her secretary roll.

"Give us five minutes Allison then stop us please," Michelle said.

Allison nodded her head and Michelle slowly leaned in. I was ready. With this being our first appointment, I didn't know what to expect. Our lips touched for only a brief moment and I instantly felt how warm and soft they were. I was enjoying every second of this wonderful feeling. It was as if time had stood still and the two of us sat and kissed while the rest of the world remained motionless. Just as I began pressing a little harder against her warm mouth, she did it. Michelle slid her thick, warm, wet tongue into my mouth then retrieved it, inviting my tongue inside her warm mouth. The feeling was indescribable and I responded as any eleven-year-old boy would.

Embarrassed for only a second, I continued exchanging tongue slides with Michelle for the full five minutes but my erection lasted much longer than that unfortunately. This was the first time that we had ever kissed and although she had been my girlfriend for over a year, we had never been alone like this. We both wanted to, but Michelle had a strong fear of getting pregnant. I know, I laugh at the thought of that too now. You see, her mother had told her that if she was to ever let a boy kiss her, she would surely get pregnant and have a baby. She also told her that she would have to stop going to school and would have to move to her grandmother's house where she would have to live and take care of her child. Michelle didn't like her grandmother much. She often spoke about how callous her grandmother was to her and how she would be thrashed for any small thing that she had done. Michelle realized very early that kissing a boy would have definitely sealed her doom. She was determined not to live in hell with her grandmother and she didn't want a child at twelve years of age. It wasn't until that summer that one of the older girls told Michelle that kissing a boy was harmless but if he stuck his penis inside her, he could cause some real damage. She assured Michelle that she had kissed plenty of boys and had never gotten pregnant from it. That was enough for Michelle to do what she's wanted to do for a long time, kiss me.

After my appointment was up I rose from the flowered print sofa and bid Michelle and Allison farewell as I was sure that they wanted to get back to the girly things that they would always do during her mother's absence. Both girls giggled as they could see in full view the bulge from my denim jeans. I produced a half smile as I hurried out of the door. This became the first of many appointments with the duration extending with every visit. Allison continued being the time monitor of our sessions and terminating them abruptly each time. Over time, I was eventually allowed to fondle Michelle's breast but for only short moments because Allison would cut that time short as well. Allison was serious about her job as receptionist and monitor and made sure that nothing happened that she didn't think Michelle would approve. There was only one occurrence when for a brief second or two Allison's mind wandered off and I was able to take advantage. As she sat daydreaming for only a short moment, I was able to get Michelle to touch me where I so desperately wanted her to, down there where all of my blood seemed to be flowing. Although a little hesitant, she too knew that Allison would interrupt this action if noticed. She quickly placed her hand on my bulge and I could tell instantly that she liked feeling it just as much as I did.

Allison, most times would only watch us, check her watch and occasionally walk over to the couch and give us a quick inspection as if she were checking for some type of sexual violation. Then as always, she would giggle sheepishly whenever my erection came into view.

I now wanted more from Michelle. We were now kissing like professionals and grinding on top of each other like porn stars. After each appointment, I would always leave with nothing but a stiff, throbbing, heated piece of flesh, aching testicles, a huge bright smile cemented to my face, and a heart full of love.

Weeks had passed and we had continued the same routine almost daily. Michelle's mother would leave for work and Allison would open the door to the horny customer standing on the front porch. I would enter, enjoy the appointment then make my exit. One evening while we were outside talking, I asked Michelle for an appointment without the presence of Allison. She informed me that she couldn't because she needed her, Allison was her guard. Her guard? She didn't need to be guarded from me, or did she?

"Why do you want to do that anyway?" she asked.

"I would just feel more comfortable if Allison wasn't standing there gawking over us like that," I responded.

"She's not gawking, she's doing her job, she's keeping track of the time."

"What do we need to keep track of the time for?"

"So we don't kiss too long."

"Kiss too long, there's no such thing and besides I want to show you something but I don't want to show you in front of her."

"Show me what?" she asked.

"You know, I want to show IT to you," I replied while pointing to my crotch and looking a little embarrassed.

"You mean, IT?"

"Yup, you do want to see it or not? You said you did."

"Uh...well yeah but how come you can't show me with Allison there? She's practically seen it anyway with it sticking out every time you leave my house," she said giggling.

"Do you want to see it or not? If you do, tell Allison to stay home tomorrow but if she answers the door, I'll know that you don't want to see it," I said then turned to leave.

I left Michelle standing there contemplating but I knew that her curiosity would surely get the best of her. She had asked me several times to see it but I would always refuse with Allison standing there gaping. I wanted to and would have shown it to her even in front of Allison but I was too ashamed. There was another reason as well that I didn't want to explain to Michelle because she would probably refuse my offer. I was a bit reluctant to show her because of how I thought she would receive it. That's right! I thought that she would possibly cringe at the sight of it. She once told me that she had seen her uncle's before and had even seen pictures of one but none like mine, I hadn't been circumcised yet and I knew she would think it was ugly.

The sun shone brightly that morning and I rose along with it. I couldn't wait to see Michelle. I got cleaned up and ate my morning bowl of cereal, took out the trash then headed outside. I walked around the block to see who was out only to find the twins out with their father in the backyard, he was teaching them how to box. With their hands stuffed inside the thick padded gloves, they swung at each other wildly. I watched on for a while before hurrying around the corner to see if Michelle's mother had left for work. But of course, to my dismay, her car was still parked in front of the house. I was growing impatient. I walked back down the alley and continued watching on as the twin's father gave them pointers on how to jab. The boys went at it again until one of the boys punched the other a little too hard and the fight broke out. Their father pulled them apart and made them take off the gloves and return inside. After my only entertainment of the morning had ended, I walked back toward the street to check on Michelle's mother's departure. I was surprised to witness her car cruising by as I approached the street. I smiled to myself then walked up the block to the house and quickly advanced toward the front door. As I neared the door, to my surprise, it opened and there stood Allison. My smile dropped. She opened the door wider and smiled at me but I did not return the gesture. She pushed the screen door open and as I entered, she exited. My heart began to pound as I realized that I would at last be alone with Michelle for the first time.

I closed the door behind Allison and walked over to the couch to sit next to Michelle.

"Alright, take it out and show it to me," She said while staring at my crotch.

"Now?" I replied.

"You said if Allison wasn't here, you'd show it to me so let me see it."

This was not how I had envisioned this happening. I wanted to kiss her and touch her breast and while it was throbbing and trying its best to burst through my tight-fitting jeans, I would unleash it and point it at her in all of its splendor and glory. I couldn't believe that she was going to rob me of my show. I had even rubbed it down with some of my dad's good hair grease so it would shine when I pulled it out. To pull it out right then I knew would only disappoint her. Flaccid, it had the appearance of a depressed, ant starved aardvark with the extra skin drooping over the head of it.

I sat next to Michelle and tried to kiss her but she only turned her head away and once again demanded to see my member. I was nervous and instead of thickening and extending in size, it was shriveling up from panic. I agreed. I stood up and unsnapped my pants as she peered straight at my zipper. Just then, the aid that I so desperately needed appeared. With the top button of her blouse undone, I could see the flawless skin of her soft breast. I wanted to touch them and envisioned how they looked. My aardvark was beginning to heat up then immediately increased in size, it was ready.

I yanked down my zipper and reached down into my underwear and pulled my hot, hard, uncircumcised penis out and placed it before her. There it was, skin pulled back, swollen so much that it was busting at the seams. It was throbbing, shining from the hair grease, and ready to explode, it was harder than a ten-cent chisel. If it had gotten any harder, I would've needed stitches. Michelle looked at my stiff pride and joy strangely. *I knew that she would think it ugly,* I thought. I opened my underwear to put it back in but before doing so she stopped me, "Wait…Can I touch it?" she asked.

"Sure," I responded while nodding rapidly."

Michelle placed her hand on the side of my throbbing flesh and gently rubbed it. It was the best feeling ever. I was so excited, I began to shake.

"Can I see yours?" I asked.

She stared at me for a moment then to my surprise, she pulled her shorts and underpants completely off. My penis grew even harder from the sight of her vagina and I instantly knew that I was going to soon need a paramedic, a doctor or even a damn army corpsman, somebody, anybody, to attend to my exploded flesh. I felt lightheaded from my excitement. I looked down at the treasure between her legs. Unlike my Aardvark area, it was covered with a beautiful thin layer of silky hair and looked like a wondrous object that I would have loved to explore. Michelle lowered herself back on the couch and I quickly mounted her. We touched each other all over as we kissed then I attempted to place myself where I thought I should be and began my first attempt of losing my virginity. I humped and pumped the side of her thigh until it was raw before I finally made my dismount. We had done it!   Well at least in my mind we had and that was just the beginning. What happened next, you're not going to believe.

<u>Chapter 2 - The Big League</u>

The inflation of my chest had finally subsided as the long summer ended. I had continued to produce skin burns on the side of each thigh and had rubbed the pelvic bone of my girlfriend that I loved raw over the entire summer. How proud was I?

School had recommenced and Michelle became inaccessible. Each day after school Michelle's mother would arrive home shortly after she did. There were no more appointments, no more thigh pokes and no more navel punctures. My sex life was over.

That year passed slowly. Days came and went and so did Michelle. With her now in junior high school, it wasn't long before the older boys saw what I had seen in Michelle years before, a red boned beauty. Michelle soon dropped me like a sack of potatoes and for the first time I had felt a hurt like no other. If only I had not repeated the third grade, maybe I would have been able to preserve her love for me. This kind of pain was something that I had never experienced in my short life time. I had been punished, gotten spankings, and had even lost relatives to death before but none of those events could remotely compare to what I was feeling at this very moment. I was crushed and it was all because of him.

He was tall, cool, muscular, and was on every varsity team at the junior high school that both he and Michelle attended. His name was Fred Eagan. He was in the ninth grade and had pounced on Michelle like a lion on a gazelle early in the school year. I had no idea why Michelle had suddenly become so distant. When she finally had decided to separate herself from me for "Mr. All American", she tried to put me down nicely. She waited for me in front of her house like she used to do most days. As I approached her, I noticed the strange look on her face. There was no smile, no excitement nor any noticeable sparks of warmth radiating from her person. I immediately knew that there was something wrong. As we stood in front of the house, she broke the news to me. She told me that her mother felt it necessary for her to focus solely on school and her studies and that hanging around "that boy" would interfere with her studies. She told me that maybe after school was out for the summer we could pick back up where we left off. I was crushed. As I turned to head home, I saw Allison peeking out from the window of Michelle's house. I headed home knowing three things; one, Allison knew that Michelle was going to dump me that day; two, Michelle would never disobey her mother; and three, it was over.

Weeks had passed before the reality of my release was revealed. Standing there talking to my "Corner partner", I was leveled! I stopped in mid-sentence as I watched from my crossing patrol corner station. I had glanced over briefly and couldn't believe my eyes. I watched on, speechless, and motionless, witnessing him walking with her. With his arm slung around her shoulders, she giggled as he talked. Every so often she would glance over across the street at me standing with my white shoulder belt on, stone faced, trying to camouflage my pain. My body went limp just thinking about the two of them. I stared at them as they continued on while I stretched my arms out keeping the smaller children from crossing the street into the oncoming traffic. I guess I hadn't paid any attention to it before but on that day, I noticed how much she had now matured. She had become a young woman, a young woman with a man.

After that day things had gotten pretty bad with me. I still loved the girl who had now moved up to the big league. The worst part about it is that everyone in the neighborhood knew about her and Fred. They would constantly remind and tease me about it every opportunity they had. Daily, without fail, I would hear how Michelle was now dating a "man" and how he was captain of the basketball, baseball and football teams at school. It sucked to be me. And just as I thought things couldn't get any worse, they did.

Several weeks later I drank a carton of milk that had soured during lunch. It turned my stomach and I began to feel very nauseous. After tossing my guts all over the floor of the classroom, I was immediately sent home. I remember climbing up Groveton Street feeling as if I had just looked up the principal's dress. I had pulled one over on them. With one spill of my guts, I had gotten the rest of the day off and with no homework. I smiled to myself and whistled as I headed up the hill approaching my neighborhood. I continued along the sidewalk on the opposite side of the street of where I'd had several appointments. As I strolled down the walk, my attention was summoned to the front door of Michelle's house. The door opened wide and to my surprise out stepped Fred. I continued my stride but kept my attention placed at the door. Fred hurried out the yard and glared over at me as he passed. Then the arrogant bastard did what I should have expected of him. In an attempt to taunt me, Fred slowed his pace as he passed by me on the opposite side of the street. He looked over at me smugly, winked his eye, smiled, then clutched his crotch before hurrying down the walk. It was the ultimate dig. An insult that he knew would slice a section from my soul and his gesture did just that! You see, without saying one word, Fred had just sent me two messages. The smug smile that he produced said only one thing, "I know she's your old girl and you still want her but now she's mine," and the clutching of his crotch was like a mores-code transmission which I read loud and clear: "And I was just inside her." My heart sank. I wanted to cry, that's right, cry but I know I would have NEVER heard the end of that. Instead, I grunted and produced a fake chuckle as if I didn't care. I don't think I fooled him at all. I'm pretty sure he knew that he had cut me deep.

Michelle stood in the doorway with her face looking exactly how she did when I used to leave her house after an appointment, guilty. The rest of her looked even worse. Her hair was a crow's nest and her clothing was hanging loosely over her sexed body. I wanted nothing else to do with her, not ever. My craving for her suddenly turned into a dark loathing and I desired her no more. I did feel some hypocrisy for only a brief moment. I reminisced on how her warm tongue explored my mouth and how soft her skin felt when I was mounted on top of her. And how at those moments she was everything to me and how I viewed her as my precious princess. Then thoughts of her with Fred interrupted those fond memories and I could see nothing but visions of him pumping between her legs with her enjoying each stroke. At that moment she was nothing to me and I now only viewed her as a slut. I wanted to kill them both.

The heated days and cool nights had soon returned. School was out again. Fred continued to visit Michelle during the summer. I had gotten over them but still, he knew how to get under my skin. Whenever he was around and I was in sight of him, he would never waste an opportunity to treat me like a kid. After all, he was now going to high school and I was only going to the seventh grade. My play brother Donald knew him from school and he and Fred were friends. They hung out occasionally. Donald would sometimes tell me things that Fred would tell him that he did to Michelle just to infuriate me. It would always work. I guess I did still love her after all of that.

Unlike Fred, there were only four times of the day when sex was on Donald's mind and that morning, afternoon, evening and night. That was all he talked about but Fred had sports. That was his love.

Donald on the other hand wanted nothing else but to be laying between some girl's legs, sweating and grinning. Most days Donald and I would have long discussions about sex. He would always try to teach me a thing or two about girls and ask me all sorts of strange questions about them. I remember one day while sitting on his front porch, Donald was rolling a huge wad of 'Play Dough' in his hand. He looked over at me smiling that big smile that he had then started in on me.

"Ok little man, it's time you fessed up," Donald said looking serious.

"Fessed up about what?" I asked.

He took a deep breath then looked deep into my eyes before asking me the question that I was sure he had already known the answer to. He leaned in and whispered, "Ever had some pussy?" he asked.

I looked up at him and said, "Of course I have! I told you that I used to get Michelle every chance that I got."

"So where did you put it?" He asked.

"Put what?" I questioned.

"Your dick, stupid!"

"I stuck it in her, where do you think I put it? You sound like the stupid one," I said chuckling

"Boy, don't make me knock your teeth out. I'll stomp you down these steps! Now where did you put it, smart ass?" he asked again.

"I don't know what you mean," I said looking at him strangely.

Donald ripped several pieces of the soft clay like substance from the wad of dough. He rolled and mashed the largest piece of dough and pushed the back of it gently with a twig until two small points protruded from it. These were supposed to be the breast of the clay figure. He then rolled a small, round piece into a ball in an effort to create a little head to attach to the soft body. Finally, he added the arms and two legs. He laid the clay figure down in front of me then repeated his question, "Where did you put it?"

Once again, I looked at him strangely. I placed my hand on my zipper just before he leaned over in my direction and grunted, "Now show me where you stuck your dick on this clay doll," he said pointing to the clump of dough laying on the porch.

I began to unzip my fly and unsurely asked, "You want me to pull my dick out and stick it in some clay?"

"No jackass, just point to where you put it!"

"Oh!"

I pulled my zipper back up and with my index finger, I pointed to where I thought I had inserted my penis into Michelle. After showing him, Donald broke out into an uncontrollable laughter. He was laughing so hard that tears streamed down the side of his cheek. He held on to his stomach as he continued to cackle.

"What in the hell is so funny?" I yelled.

"Man, that ain't it! Boy, you haven't had no pussy, maybe pussy bone but definitely not pussy. Actually, it looks like you might have screwed the hell out of her navel," Donald said before starting to laugh again.

"Well if that's not it, where in the hell is it then?" I asked looking somewhat embarrassed.

Donald looked at me still chuckling a bit and shaking his head. He picked up a small piece of twig from the step and pushed it in between the clay figure's legs.

"That's it, that's it right there. That's where you wanna be! That's the only place you wanna hang out, any place else... is dry dock."

I looked at the clay figure then back at Donald before finally realizing that I had never actually done it. I had never had sex! Donald stopped laughing then looked at me as if to apologize. It was as if he suddenly felt sorry for me or something. He placed his hand on my shoulder then punched me on the arm with his other hand. "Don't worry man, we'll get you some. At least this time, you'll know where to put it," he said in an attempt to get in one more dig.

I thought about how I had always thought that although Fred had her now, I had had her first, NOT! I thought about her looking up at him, into his eyes as he pleasured her and felt sick to my stomach. I felt like such a fool and what made matters even worse was I suddenly realized, "*Damn, I'm still a virgin!*" After all the bragging I had done to all who would listen. I told my buddies, my sister, my pastor…I mean, I didn't tell him that I had been getting butt naked and drilling inside Michelle's insides, I just asked him if it was a sin to have sex at my age. Anyway, I told the man that ran the dry cleaners, the television repair guy, and of course Reggie, the guy who drove the ice cream truck. He was so cool. Reggie would always talk to us boys while we were buying ice cream from him. He would always ask us about our girlfriends and most times, if we were getting any. I would always be the first to say that I was getting it every day, even after Michelle was with Fred. He'd laugh then ring the bell on his truck a few more times and then laugh some more. He'd always tell us to wrap our little peckers up in anything if you didn't have a condom before we got burned or some girl got pregnant then he would laugh once again then the ringing of the bell would follow. He was a cool guy with a cool job. I remember thinking that I wanted to be just like him when I grew up and that I was definitely going to have a successful career as an ice cream man.

Chapter 3 - The Real Deal

The days passed and there was little to no change in my young sex life. Donald however was humping everything that moved and everybody knew it. When he would come over to our house, the fish in the aquarium, the fingerling included, would literally still themselves. For they too knew that if any movement at all, even only an inch, could quite possibly draw the attention of the two legged, sex craved menace. And in doing this, they too would become at risk of possibly losing their dignity or finding themselves in a very compromising position. For he would surely bring an entire new meaning to the word "fingerling."

It was now autumn and the leaves were drifting colorfully from their branches. They had already begun to blanket the grass and the asphalt roads. The cooler temperatures had arrived and the sun dissipated from the sky earlier than in the weeks before. Night had fallen by six o'clock and of course, all of the kids that had "just after dusk" curfews now had to be home even earlier. The streets would begin to empty soon after the street lights illuminated. Fortunately for me, I was not one of those kids. My mother had a strict indoor/outdoor policy. Once outside, I was to remain outside unless I had to use the bathroom, eat or had injured myself. Actually, I would have had to sustain a close-to-life threatening injury in order to re-enter the house during the day. This injury would require bleeding, a broken or fractured bone, a missing limb or fragments of brain seeping from my skull. Oh yeah, my mother was very tough and strict when it came to running in and out of her house. My outside privileges were better than most as long as I was inside of the house before my sisters. This wasn't a very challenging task to accomplish. Normally they would be visiting over at one of their friend's houses. They would hang out listening to music, sneaking cigarettes, and were never in a hurry to come home. I was usually one of the first kids to go in for the night.

I can remember one particular night as if it were yesterday. In fact, I'll never forget that night, not ever! That was the best night of my life! On that night I learned so much about life. It was the night that I learned what it meant to become a man. I can still remember patrolling the neighborhood that night. I wasn't in a rush to go inside and was only in search of company. As I slowly walked by the alley, I could hear my name being called in the distance. I immediately recognized the voice, it was Donald. He was sitting on the porch with Sylvia. Sylvia lived just across the street from Donald and ever since she could breathe and had the use of all of her legs, she chased after him. Donald wouldn't even give her the time of day until almost about a year ago. It was then that Sylvia had seemed to shed her short, pudgy, dusty little girl body and began slipping on her breasts and butt outfit. Still a somewhat stout girl, she was now the new owner of a very shapely figure and an attractive face. She had now began catching the eye of most of the boys her age and older. This was the start of her development into womanhood and her new womanly figure quickly slowed Donald's running. After his pace had come to a standstill, it was already assumed by all that Donald was having his way with her. It was assumed because she had always chased after him and with her new body, he now kept her by his side. She seemed to only like two people in the world, Donald and her father. And to her father, she was the apple of his eye. This was quite problematic for Donald. You see, Sylvia's father was one of the most unpleasant men in the neighborhood or in this case, I had ever seen. He was very strict and hard on Sylvia. In fact, he was so strict that it was very seldom that Sylvia was even permitted to leave the yard of their home. He was so heartless and cruel that even when allowed to leave the yard, Sylvia had to be inside the gate by the time the street lights were on. If not, he would walk around the entire neighborhood with his belt in hand and once found, Sylvia would be spanked all the way home. She could never seem to outrun him either. Needless to say, if the street lights flickered at twelve o'clock noon due to a malfunction, Sylvia would rush home in a panic.

Sylvia, now in the ninth grade but looking much more mature for her age was very sheltered because of her father's strict rules. He didn't permit her to attend sleepovers, parties, after school dances or sporting events of any kind and definitely... NO BOYS! He was making sure that his little chubby princess remained untarnished and chaste for marriage. Donald was the only boy that she was allowed to really associate with since he lived just across the street from them and had known Sylvia practically since she was born. Yeah, I know what you're thinking... it didn't make sense to me either. Why would her father trust his precious little ladybug with the horniest toad in the pond? Well let's just say, her dad gave himself more credit than Donald did. Sylvia's father had known Donald since he too was just a little tyke. He and Donald's father were very good friends and would often go fishing together and would even take Donald along with them at times. Her dad knew that Donald not only respected him but feared him as well. He seemed to take great pride in knowing that Donald would not dare cross the line with his Sylvia. I also knew that Donald wouldn't cross her callous father too...but his pecker however, well, it had no conscience nor fear. It was always willing to take a chance even if it would put Donald's life in jeopardy.

I walked over to the fence and spoke to Sylvia then asked Donald what he wanted. He looked at me and smiled while pointing adjacent to the porch where he and Sylvia sat. I turned and looked across the street. There standing under the flickering street light near her fence was none other than Michelle and Allison. Michelle was balled up in her thick sweater, laughing and talking to her best friend and neighbor who now towered over her more than ever. It appeared that Allison had gotten even taller over the school year. I looked at Donald and nonchalantly shrugged my shoulders before turning to resume my neighborhood patrol. Sure, I still desired Michelle and wanted nothing more than for her to call out to me and run over into my arms. Yes, she was still a slut, a harlot, and the same whore that broke my young heart into pieces... but a whoring, heartbreaking slut that I still loved and wanted. Suddenly as I turned and without warning, Donald yelled out my name then laughed loudly. I quickly turned around in the direction of his bellowing voice and peered at him angrily just before hearing the sweet angelic voice call out to me. "Bobby is that you?"

I looked over toward the two girls then back at Donald. Still submerged in laughter, he and Sylvia rose from the porch.

"Hey Michelle, yeah, it's me, how ya doin'?" I yelled back over to her.

"Boy, get yourself on over here. I haven't seen you since forever."

I paused for a brief moment, looked back over at Donald who was still chuckling then eased my way across the street. And of course, Donald and Sylvia soon followed. I wasn't surprised by this action from the two, Donald just wanted to come over to instigate and torture me and Sylvia just wanted to make sure that Donald behaved himself. I walked up to Michelle, the girl that I now wanted to despise but couldn't.

"Hey, how you doin' Allison?" I asked to our old timekeeper and "Cock-blocker."

"I'm doing good, where have you been hiding?" She replied while producing a strange smile.

"Oh, I've been around. I mostly hang out down the hill with the Johnson brothers."

"Oh ok, so that's why I haven't seen you?" Allison asked.

"Yeah, I guess."

"Yeah, he's been hiding from us around here for some reason. I guess he's too good to hang out with us anymore," Donald yelled out as he neared the conversation.

"No, we do a lot of stuff down the hill. We made a go-cart last month, that was pretty cool. You know, play ball and stuff like that," I answered in my defense.

Donald decided to cut to the chase and smacked one right out of the ballpark. "Oh and all this time I thought it was because you were still heartbroken from losing Michelle," he said smirking.

I looked at Donald as if I could have punched him right in the mouth but remained silent. We both knew that I wasn't going to do anything. I knew that an action like that would be nothing but an act of suicide on my part and definitely wouldn't turn out in my favor so I just sucked it up and tried to work through it. "Uh, oh no, I was ok with that. I mean, she's older than me anyway," I mumbled while trying to conceal my embarrassment.

"What's that got to do with anything? And you're not even a year apart!" Sylvia said grinning.

I wanted to slap the hell out of her too but she too, was much bigger than me and would have probably beaten me beyond recognition so once again I took it.

"Look, I gotta go. It was good seeing you Michelle, you too Allison," I said while throwing my hand up in an attempt to wave.

I turned and with my head lowered, I retreated back across the street. I was humiliated once again. As I stepped onto the curb Michelle called out to me. "Bobby, wait up."

I stopped and turned and watched as she rushed over to where I stood.

"I'll see you tomorrow Allison," she yelled to her girlfriend as she trotted across the street.

I could hear Allison smack her lips together as she snatched herself around and stormed up to her front door filled with anger. I guess she wasn't ready to go in yet. That or either she wanted to hang out with us but I wanted no part of that. I hadn't seen Michelle for a while and was feeling sort of special because she appeared to want to spend some time with me. Boy, was I a sucker.

Donald and Sylvia walked back over to his porch. They stood there gawking at Michelle and I in anticipation of more entertainment. It would have tickled them both pink if they could hear Michelle shoot me down just once more during our conversation. They both stood there whispering and giggling quietly enough to continue to eavesdrop on us.

"Where you going?" Michelle asked.

"Uh… I… I was just going for a walk," I said.

"Oh, well would it be ok if I walked with you? I mean, as long as you don't go too far."

"Oh no, I'm just walking around the block, that's all."

"Ok, then let's go," she said cheerfully while taking hold of my arm.

I wasn't sure what this was all about. Maybe Michelle felt sorry for me because I'm sure she had heard about all of the teasing that I had been battered with after the break up. Or maybe Fred told her about the gestures that he had made to me outside her house after he had just polished her off. Maybe she knew just how much she had hurt me and no matter how much I tried to hide it, it bled through like a dark marker on a sheet of thin construction paper.

We talked and laughed as we strolled through the neighborhood. She told me how mature I now looked and that I would always be her first boyfriend. I was kind of flattered by that but not as much as I would have if she had said first lover. It took everything that I had inside to conceal the huge smile that was so desperately trying to smear itself across my face. I almost told her how much I missed her too but my pride blocked all of those kinds of comments too. I was not going to give her that satisfaction. She told me that if she and Fred were to ever break up that she wanted me to be her boyfriend again. Well I knew that wasn't ever going to happen but I just nodded in agreement. After all, he was a football player, a good one at that and all the girls wanted him but he wanted Michelle. Yeah right, like she's ever gonna give that up. What would you have done if you were her? Wait, don't answer that, I already feel bad enough.

I walked Michelle back to her gate and she kissed me on the cheek then told me that she still loved me. I wanted to kiss her but could see sergeant Allison peeking out at us from her bedroom window. I knew she was part Native American but I didn't know that she was part of the "Cock Blocker" tribe. Just as I was about to walk away, Michelle leaned in and gently pressed her lips against mine. Immediately the appointment memories returned. I quickly deduced that an army of ants must have been in the near area because that damn aardvark of mine was warming and rising up. It had been awakened and was already stretching. Michelle looked down at my now bulging denim jeans and began to smile.

"You haven't changed a bit huh?" she said.

I didn't reply, I couldn't. I merely smiled at her.

"Hey, remember how we used to have those appointments?" she asked chuckling.

"Yeah, I remember, how could I forget? I can still remember our first kiss and how you started moving your tongue around in my mouth," I said smiling.

"Yes, but it's better now," She said.

"Oh yeah?"

"Yep," She answered proudly.

"Yeah right, that's just what I want to hear, that the guy you're with now taught you how to kiss even better, you BITCH!" I thought to myself. I know, I wanted to say it out loud but I still loved her.

I kissed Michelle on the cheek once again, waved to Allison who was still gawking through the curtains of her window then headed back across the street. Donald and Sylvia were no longer on the porch. I did notice that Sylvia's dad's car was still vacant from the parking space in front of their house. I immediately assumed that she was probably inside Donald's house with him getting another dosage of the ole hot beef injection. I wanted to give them both a piece of my mind for embarrassing me earlier but knew that it would now have to wait until the following day.

I walked down the hill now heading for home when the abrupt movement caught my eye. I wasn't quite sure what it was at first but my curiosity had quickly gotten the best of me. I slowly neared the house from where the strange noise came. There was another quick movement then I heard a rustling sound coming from between the two screened porches of the adjoining homes. I froze but looked on. There was someone between the porches of the houses. Before I made my move to defend my neighborhood, I took a second to prepare myself. I was ready. I firmly planted my foot and positioned myself in the opposite direction for a quick take-off then yelled out, "Hey! What are you doing in there?"

The response was as sudden as my planed escape, "Bobby shut the hell up!" The voice whispered.

"Donald, is that you?" I whispered in return as I inched nearer.

"Shhhhhh, come here and shut the hell up."

I eased between the bushes and through the narrow opening of the walls of the porches. Inside I found Donald standing there with Sylvia. He looked at me and smiled while she merely stood there looking at me shamefully. I had no idea what was going on so of course being an inquisitive twelve-year-old, I just asked.

"What are you guys doing in here?"

"What in the hell do you think fool and keep your damn voice down," Donald whispered.

It wasn't until I had noticed the absence of Sylvia's jeans and the quilted blanket of shame and embarrassment that was stitched together with a thin thread of anger, did I realized what was actually happening. I looked at her then immediately stared at her crotch. Don't judge, like I said... I was twelve years old for crying out loud!

I gasped after observing that her vaginal area was completely covered with hair and a lot of it. More hair than I had ever seen around one in my short lifetime. And I'm sure that I don't even need to mention this but yes, that damn aardvark quickly returned and immediately shot into "seek and destroy" mode. I knew both Donald and Sylvia would have killed me if I tried to touch her hair covered pocket so I just stood there frozen and marveled at its splendor. I couldn't take my eyes off of it. Suddenly, my concentration was interrupted by her high-pitched whispering voice, "Hurry up and get an eye full then get out!" she grunted angrily.

I quickly snapped out of it and tried to gather my composure but it was too late. My flesh was so hard that it was hurting. It pushed uncontrollably to release itself from its captivity. My mind raced as I schemed on how I too could feel her.

"Ok, get out," She whispered.

I looked at Donald then asked quietly, "Can I watch?"

Donald looked at me and smiled, "I don't care if she doesn't."

"Hell no, I'm not gonna do it while he's standing there gawking at us like some little pervert, this isn't a show. Now get out!" she barked.

Donald walked up to her and stood close, pressing his body firmly against hers. Now trying to prove to me how in control he was, he started in on her.

"Come on baby, it'll be just like he's not here and besides, we'll probably be teaching the little bastard a thing or two, come on now."

Sylvia looked around Donald's shoulder and peered at me angrily. Donald quickly placed one of his hands on the side of her face and guided it back over directly in front of his and began kissing Sylvia. He worked his tongue in and around the inside of her mouth until she began to breathe heavily. She slowly began opening her legs and Donald slowly slid his hand down between her legs then eased his fingers inside her. She moaned slightly but then welcomed them. That aardvark, even though I thought that it could get any harder, did. It now felt like a hard rubber tube with water stuck inside it waiting to be released. I tell you, it was ready to blow!

Sylvia had now opened her legs wider. Donald unsnapped his pants and dropped them and his underwear down to his knees. He maneuvered between her legs then positioned his stiff erection against her opening. As he began to push inside her, she gasped. He paused for only a second then turned and looked at me and smiled. I smiled back and nodded. What can I say, I was a young nasty bastard and at that moment, Donald as well as I, both knew that he was surely my hero.

With a quick thrust, Donald pushed all of himself into Sylvia. Then he continued his pumping for several minutes. He was now in "thrust factor three," humping harder and faster than ever. I had nearly passed out from all the excitement. I took a deep breath, collected myself then watched on as Donald gave one last hard thrust inside the thick girl. He yanked himself out of her and grabbed tightly on to his still hard erected penis then suddenly began to grunt and jerk.

"What in the hell happened?" I wondered. *Maybe he hit a chipped bone up inside her and it punctured his pecker or something. Or maybe something up in there cut him,* I thought. I wasn't sure what had caused such a reaction from Donald like that but I watched on as he continued convulsing and jerking. He was perspiring and still twitching. Thinking that maybe he could have had an epileptic seizure or something I stepped toward my convulsing friend but soon noticed him calming. He was alright. It had appeared that he had healed.

After catching his breath, Donald leaned over and kissed Sylvia then looked at me and whispered, "Now that's how it's done."

"Are you alright? Did you get cut or something, what happened that made jerk like that?" I asked forgetting to whisper.

"Shhhhhh, don't you know anything stupid? I came!"

"You what?"

"I came, idiot! That's what happens when you become a man. You stroke it then you shoot your juices and it feels so good," Donald said proudly.

"Oh, so that's supposed to happen?" I asked.

"Hell yeah, and if it doesn't, you'll be pissed."

"Well I think I'd rather be pissed because... well that just looks too painful for me."

"That's what you say now but once you've experienced that first one... that's all you'll look forward to," Donald said as he continued to collect himself.

"For her too?" I asked turning my eyes over toward Sylvia.

"What do you mean?" Donald asked.

"For her, I mean, I didn't see her twitching and jerking, she doesn't get to have that same feeling?" I asked while once again turning my sights to Sylvia.

"Oh nah, they just like it when you stick it in them, that's all. They don't do that, that's just for us guys," Donald said arrogantly.

"Yeah, you'll understand when you get some," Sylvia said while reaching for her underwear.

"Well how about now, I can understand now. Now is as good a time as any," I said while trying to calm the aardvark.

With a harsh look, Sylvia looked at me and bluntly said, "Hell no! You won't be getting any of this you little perv so you might as well take your horny little self home and put some cold water on that thing!"

"Well why not, you gave Donald some?" I inquired.

"That's because Donald is my boyfriend," she responded proudly.

"Does your father know that he's your boyfriend?" I asked with eyebrows raised.

"No, and he won't either."

"Well, he will if I tell him," I said standing far enough out of harm's way.

"I wish to hell you would, I'd kick your ass throughout this entire neighborhood," Sylvia said angrily.

"I just want a little bit. Then neither of us will have anything to worry about. You won't have to worry about your father knowing that you have a boyfriend and I won't have to worry about getting my ass kicked when I tell him."

I didn't care about getting my ass kicked. That was only a small price to pay to stick my still ever so hard meat and gristle between all that hair. Finally, being a man of his word, Donald interrupted our debate.

"Aww girl, go on and give the little bastard some. You know he'll tell too, and your father will kill us both. Well you, he'd just beat for weeks but me, he'd really kill. How bad could it be and you know he'll be quick. I don't want to have to deal with your father so if you really care anything about me, about us, you'll just do it."

Sylvia looked at Donald then at me then pulled her panties back off. "Aww come on you little dog and you'd better be quick about it. I can't believe this and you'd better NOT tell anybody about this either."

I rushed over to where Sylvia stood but still kept a little distance just in case she had changed her mind. I believe my willy was out before I could reach down to take it out. It must have unzipped and unsnapped my pants on its own and released itself. I guess it hadn't changed its mind. I inched closer to Sylvia with my pants lowered and looked over at Donald smiling. He gave me the thumbs up as I pressed forward.

"Wait! What's wrong with that thing?"

"What do you mean?" I asked.

"What's it's have, a stocking cap on it or something? It's like it's in a sack or wearing a turtle neck or something," Sylvia whispered while pointing at the extra skin drooping over the head of my penis.

I looked down at my still throbbing penis unembarrassed and gave her a detailed medical explanation of its condition, "That's just how it is."

"Come on girl, stop stalling, it's fine just hurry up," Donald chimed in.

With that, I quickly inched even closer. With Sylvia being taller than me, I was now pressed against her and on the tip of my toes trying to enter her but just couldn't reach.

"You're gonna have to lay down, you're too tall for me to do it like this," I said nicely.

"Well you'd better find something to stand on because I'm not laying down on that dirty ass ground," She responded harshly.

"There's nothing here."

"Oh well, then I guess you won't be getting your little turtle neck wearing prick wet this evening huh?"

I looked over at Donald for assistance and of course, he didn't let me down.

"Look here, how about I lay my jacket down? He can lay his down too," Donald suggested.

"Hell no, this ground is dirty!" she yelled.

"Shhhhh, girl what are trying to do, get us caught?" Donald whispered forcefully.

"What are you trying to do?" she replied.

"I'm just trying to keep me from getting shot and your ass from getting whipped by your dad. You're going to be laying on our jackets. You could have been done with this by now if you would just stop all of this bitchin'. Just lay your ass down and give this little jackass some of that stuff so we can all go home and won't have to worry about his little ass snitchin' to your evil ass father. So, let's do this!" Donald demanded.

Sylvia angrily snatched the jackets from Donald's hand. She spread them over the cold earth then quickly lowered her thick body on top of them. I quickly mounted her and started pumping like a mad man. I maneuvered around trying to find the opening that Donald had showed me on the clay model but was still unsuccessful. Suddenly without warning, Sylvia reached down and grabbed the shaft of my penis then placed it at the warm opening that Donald had just penetrated.

"Here, now hurry up! I swear, it'll take your dumb ass all day just trying to find it," she grunted.

Like a bullet, I pushed inside. Her insides felt slippery, wet and so warm. The warmth of it penetrated through skin and flesh of my stiff shaft. Her soft hair brushing against me as I pushed felt indescribable. I fell in love with that warmth on that day. It had just become my new best friend.

I pumped on top of Sylvia until she began to try to push me off. That was not an easy task for her. I was dug in like a leach.

"Alright, that's enough you little freak, get off of me!" she grunted.

"Just a little more," I whispered.

"No, you've had enough."

"I'll tell."

"You said you wouldn't if I gave you some and you've gotten some, now get the hell off of me!"

"Just a few more minutes," I begged.

"Aww, give 'em just a couple more pumps then I'll get him off of you. As a matter of fact, give it to him hard and he'll stop," Donald chimed in.

With that, Sylvia started pumping and grinding back against me. It felt even more exciting. She was moving in every direction possible. Then she suddenly slowed in her movements. She started grinding me in the same direction and I followed her movement. At that point she stopped complaining. It was as if she gave in to the idea of giving me some. We moved in rhythm and harmony. I was loving it and Sylvia seemed to be enjoying it too. This went on for a few minutes more then she, same as Donald had done earlier, Sylvia began to shake and twitch. I thought I had done something wrong. Especially after I began to feel the rush of hot wetness cover my penis. Shortly after, Sylvia stopped moving. She looked at me strangely and I smiled at her. I was still ready to continue but she had a look of contentment, relaxation, relief and gratitude.   She was no longer angry or complaining. I continued with my pumping and she lay still letting me.

I could feel his arms wrapping around my waist in his attempt to pull me from off of her. I hung on as tight as I could before I could no longer keep my grip. Donald had finally snatched me off from my new found favorite spot. Sylvia's shoulders were deeply scratched as a result of me clinging on but still, she said nothing.

I stood there next to Donald panting. He rubbed my back in an attempt to settle me, still whispering, "Whoa tiger, whoa, calm down."

I was still ready. Since I had not yet reached puberty, I had not experienced the convulsing and twitching which meant that I could pump all day.

Sylvia pulled herself up and got dressed. I retrieved Donald's and my own soiled covered jackets from the ground. I passed Donald his jacket and he quickly brushed the earth from it. We eased out from between the porches and back up to Donald's porch. Sylvia didn't say much afterwards either, she merely collected herself and said that she was going home. I thanked her and promised that I wouldn't tell anybody, especially her dad. I smiled at Donald and thanked him too. He gave me the "thumbs up" once again and I headed for home whistling.

The next morning was a glorious one. I ate my bowl of cereal, got cleaned up, did my chores around the house then quickly rushed outside. As I strolled through the neighborhood, I told everybody that I saw about what had happened the night before. Everybody now knew that I was no longer a virgin. Yes, they all now viewed Sylvia as a tramp but that didn't tarnish my reputation any, I was no longer a virgin. Oh yeah, seems that Donald was wrong about what he told me that night, girls do get that same feeling that he had gotten on that night. It wasn't just for us guys. Sylvia, for the first time had experience this feeling, with me. That night she had experienced her very first orgasm and with me, go figure. I was a satisfaction machine and didn't even know it. Sylvia enjoyed experiencing that feeling so much, I helped her experience this sensation countless more times over the next year. Even while she was still going with Donald. She asked me not to tell him so I never did. I threw my jacket down between those porches every time she requested. She was always appreciative as was I.

Chapter 4 - Robyn

The rustling and loud slamming sounds of metal lockers carried throughout the narrow hallway. The kids were digging through their lockers and talking loudly as they fooled about just before their next class. This was the fourth week of school. Now in junior high, I felt like a little man. I stood there digging around in my locker when I heard her voice. It was Michelle. My heart began to do what it always did when I heard her voice; it pounded heavily in an attempt to escape my chest to be near her. I turned slowly only to catch a quick glimpse of her as she walked by smiling. "Hi Bobby!" she said.

My heart raced and began to beat even harder. I could already start to feel the blood rushing through my groin. I still wanted her.

The smile that I had received from Michelle was one of hope for me, after all, I too was now walking amongst the older generation. I now felt like a man. That ray of hope soon dissipated as I watched her walk down the hallway to the awaiting arms of yet another football player. It was hopeless. Once more I had decided to forget about the woman that I still, for some reason, couldn't shake out of my head. She had my mind and my heart still tangled in the cobwebs of the afterthoughts of our once vibrant but unsuccessful love making. I so desperately wanting to redeem myself, especially now that I knew where to put it.

Throughout the rest of the year, I made countless attempts at satisfying my thirst for lust but no one would heed the call. It wasn't until summer once again that I found myself back in the saddle, her name was Robyn. Who would have ever thought that after all of my unsuccessful attempts, the answer to my prayers would come by chance? I was merely mailing a letter for crying out loud. I had walked up the block to the postbox to deposit my mom's monthly bundle of mail and suddenly from out of nowhere her majestic voice called out to me.

"Are you mailing me a letter?" she asked sarcastically.

I turned and looked at her bright cheerful face and only waved to her. She strolled up to the gate and I walked over to meet her.

"So, you don't have anything to do today except give me a hard time huh?" I asked smiling.

She reached out and pushed my shoulder and giggled.

"That's right! That's all I have to do today and if it bothers you that much, I might just have to put in some overtime," she jokingly replied.

The stern look that I had forcefully displayed lasted only seconds before we both erupted into laughter. I had always thought that she was a sweet and funny girl but it was not until then that she appeared as something on my lust menu. I was somewhat cautious about making any advancements toward Robyn because as fate would have it, she was also close friends with Allison, you know, the "timekeeper" that lived next door to Michelle.

Robyn was a tall girl. In fact, she towered me by several inches. She wasn't very attractive facially in my opinion nor was she what I would have considered ugly either. Her body was what did it for me, it was very mature. She had full hips that complemented her nice round backside. Her breasts were like nice ripe, round melons that were ready for the picking. And it was known throughout the neighborhood that Robyn wasn't like most of the other girls, she kept her legs closed tight! Stanley Gibson was the only guy ever to have his way with the voluptuous teen. He had lived just down the block from her and had been her boyfriend since the third grade. Stanley and his family had just moved to North Carolina and he vowed to return and marry Robyn. As I examined her womanly figure and calculated how many years it would be before poor Stanley would even have a driver's license, I started in on her. I knew that a long meaningful courtship would have to take place with Robyn long before I would even receive my first kiss from her but she was worth it.

Robyn and I became engrossed in a rated "G" relationship. If I tried to make any physical advancement whatsoever toward her, she would just merely giggle and ask me if that was all that I ever thought about. Yes, it was but that answer would never get me any closer to quenching my sexual thirst and I was now parched beyond belief. Our courtship was just beginning but I was already feeling pretty sure that the undertaking of this task was not a wise one and the results were sure to be unfavorable. Though Robyn did like having me as her boyfriend, it was not enough to inspire her to pull not even one leg out of her panties. I was already getting very frustrated with this undertaking and figured that I had bit off more than I could chew. It became very apparent that there were no doors to be opened by me to get to this woman. I was missing something. I thought long and hard about how I could pull her in closer then it finally hit me, her sensitivity. With her stern facade and her sharp tongue, Robyn had one weakness. Although she did not want to admit this to herself, Robyn was very sensitive. I remembered how the tears would well up in her eyes each time we spoke of Stanley. She still missed him and displayed it with every mention of his name. This was it. This would be my sexual vehicle, my lure, her sensitivity.

Days had passed and I hadn't seen Robyn. I had taken some time away from her to devise my plan. I thought about the "I only have six months to live" routine but knew it would never fly with Robyn. She would have told me to make sure I picked a nice suit to be buried in, knowing her. A brain tumor sounded as if it would have some good booty bargaining power but she would have told me that I shouldn't get too excited in that case because it might make my head explode. There was nothing that I could think of. I had decided to give up on Robyn. Her wall was just too solid and extremely high to climb. It was now time to erase all lustful thoughts of this girl from my twisted, little horny mind.

The following morning, I felt like my old self. The frustration was gone. I had cleared my mind of Robyn and as always thoughts of Michelle re-entered into the empty space that Robyn had temporally occupied. I was back to wondering who she was seeing now, if she ever thought of me or if I would ever have another chance with her. With Michelle heavy on my mind, I stepped through the back door and trotted down the steps of the porch with a full bag of trash in hand. As I reached the litter container, I looked up toward the house where Michelle lived. Now, I never believed in fate until that very moment. There, walking up the hill was the full-figured body that I knew very well. I waved to her. She waved and as if she had read my mind while heading in my direction. I dropped the trash filled sack into the container and walked through the gate and towards her. We met at the end of the alley. She smiled at me and to my surprise, hugged me. My heart immediately warmed up to her but I had overheated even faster down in the boiler room between my legs. She seemed different, kinder and more attached to me than ever before. I looked at her then placed my hand on her shoulder. "You ok?"

She looked over at me with sadness resting in her eyes then replied in a sweet, soft voice, "Well, not really."

"What's wrong?"

"It's my grandmother, she's very ill. My parents have gone to see her at the hospital; she was rushed there last night. They wouldn't take us with them because my dad says it might upset her even more. My sister went over to Allison's house because she didn't want to be home sitting around thinking and worrying about my grandmother all day. So, I decided to take a walk hoping it would help me feel better. If something were to happen to her, I'd just die, I swear I would."

"Don't talk like that and besides, if you died, where would that leave me?"

Now, I know you all are going to view me as some kind of huge jerk but so what. That's right, instead of my compassion kicking in over the unfortunate situation with her grandmother; my lust booster had just kicked into overdrive. I mean, come on, you would have thought the same thing. I figured, empty house, parents gone, sister away and a lonely walking girl standing in front of me in need of consoling. You know you would have thought the same way if you were me. Anyway, I gave her a hug and looked deep into her eyes and spoke to her as caringly as I possibly could.

"Hey, give me a second, you shouldn't be alone right now. I'll walk with you."

All of my thoughts of Michelle were thrown in the trash container along with the litter filled bag that I had chucked. Robyn needed me and I knew that this was an opportunity of a lifetime.

I ran inside while she rested against the fence waiting. I rushed upstairs and kicked off my slippers and popped on my socks and shoes. As I zoomed by my mother's room I yelled out. "I'm going outside Ma!"

Down the stairs I went taking two steps at a time. I sped through the house and back out the door to my awaiting damsel in distress. She smiled at me and gave me another hug before we began our stroll.

We walked around the entire neighborhood talking about anything but her grandmother. I wanted her mind completely free from her sadness and nothing else but the kindness and compassion that I was displaying to blanket any thoughts of grandma. As we neared her house I used an old technique that Donald had taught me some time ago. I looked at her then placed my hand up to my throat while whispering. "All of this walking has made me thirsty as anything. Do you suppose when we get to your house I could trouble you for a glass of water?"

Robyn looked at me suspiciously for a brief moment then smiled and nodded. "You'll have to wait on the porch though, because my parents will kill me if I have company while they're not home."

"No problem," I replied.

After approaching the house, we walked up to the front door where I leaned back against the porch railing and folded my arms as I waited patiently. Robyn proceeded inside the house to fetch the glass of water that I had requested. Shortly after Robyn had disappeared, she returned with the tall cold glass of water. Although I wasn't thirsty, I accepted the glass from Robyn then quickly gulped the water down until the glass was empty. Knowing that this would probably be the only opportunity, I began my offense.

"I know you're probably wonderin'…" I started.

Just as I had begun my assault on her the telephone rang. Robyn rushed inside and answered it after only two rings.

"Hello," She said then paused as the voice on the other end spoke. After a moment, Robyn joined back in the conversation.

"Alright Daddy, I will and give grandma my love… alright I will… yes… alright then. Bye, Daddy."

Robyn sat the phone back on its cradle and returned to the porch.

"How's your grandma?" I asked.

"About the same. That was my dad. He was just checking on us, said that they'll probably be up there most of the day and that I should probably fix something for dinner because they'll be late."

This was fate I tell you. This was happening just too perfect. It was like the moon was in Aquarius while Jupiter was aligned with Mars or whatever astrological symbol makes people come together.

"Most of the day? I can't stand out here all day. I'll tell you what, why don't you start your dinner and I'll come back in a few hours or so. We can sit on the porch after you're done with dinner," I said trying to push her just a little.

"You're not going to leave me, are you?"

"Well it is pretty hot out here. We could always go down to my house and hang out but you wouldn't be able to start your dinner for a while."

Robyn stared at me for a second then looked in both directions of the street and in that instant I knew. I knew that she was about to utter those words that I longed to hear. She looked at me with a devious grin. "I guess you could come in for a little while."

This was it! This was the moment that I had been waiting for. We both scanned the area for a brief moment then I quickly stepped inside. She led me into the living room and sat down on the plastic covered couch. I sat down close beside her. We looked at each other and smiled as if we both knew that we were doing something mischievous.

"So, what should we do, seeing that we have practically all day?" I asked making sure she knew what I was getting at.

"Oh, I don't know. We could watch television," she replied with a smile.

"I don't see a T.V. down here. Where is it, in your room?"

"There's one in the basement and its cooler down there too."

We looked in each other's eyes and I peeled my arm from the sticky plastic which held it captive and placed it around her.

"Yeah, we could go downstairs and I could turn on the television. You could watch whatever you wanted while I start dinner."

Of course, I wasn't trying to let this moment slip away. As far as I was concerned, both she and her sister could starve today. I had an even bigger hunger that needed to be fed. I've made it all the way inside and this seems to still be an unwinnable battle.

After ignoring her proposition, I gently placed my hand on the side of her neck and stroked her warm skin slowly. Now, expecting her to give me a short sermon on her principles before escorting me to the front door, Robyn did the unexpected. She turned and looked deeply into my eyes just before she leaned in. Yes, that's right! She leaned over closer to my face and closed her eyes with her sweet thick lips puckered. I guess she figured that if she gave me a kiss I would be satisfied. She didn't realize that she was sitting next to "Mr. Horny" himself and that would be a negative.

I leaned in and our lips touched. I slowly slid my tongue between her lips and she accepted it. We kissed passionately for a moment then suddenly like a locomotive, I could feel the warm breath rush from her nostrils. She was heating up. I moved in closer and without warning, I placed my hand on the back of her neck and began to kiss her even harder and more passionately. She was now breathing harder than ever. I placed my hand on her thigh. My first thought was to slide it between her legs but before doing so, my memory kicked in. Thoughts of Donald lecturing me about foreplay jumped into my mind.

Now moving my tongue freely around her mouth, I reached up and placed my hand firmly on one of Robyn's breast. Her nipple felt like a bullet. It was rock hard and stiff as a board and she was now panting heavier than ever. As for me, I was hoping that the stitching in my Levi's jeans was strong enough to contain this missile that was about to launch.

Minutes had passed but they felt more like hours. It was time. I slid in even closer to her. Without giving it a second thought and her any warning, I did it. I released the soft, round, handful of flesh and eased my hand down between Robyn's legs. She did just as I suspected she would. She grabbed my hand and moved back over. Her facial expression had completely changed. She just stared at me for a moment then rose up from the couch.

"Maybe we should go and watch some television," she said coldly.

Damn! I knew it was too good to be true. Well of course I couldn't stand at that very instant. I had a boner that you could strike a match off of. I did what any other red blooded American male would do. I asked for another glass of water.

Robyn picked up my glass from off the coffee table where I had placed it. With the same odd look on her face, she walked into the kitchen.

"Come on, you can drink your water downstairs," she said while gesturing with her hand for me to follow.

After hearing this, I quickly reached down into my pants and pulled my heated bundle of flesh up and tucked it under the fastener of my jeans.   I stood up and made another adjustment before heading toward the kitchen. It was like walking with a human stick shift and I felt like I was in third gear.

I stepped into the kitchen and Robyn handed me the cold glass of water that I had no desire to drink. This time it was filled to the brim. She motioned me to follow once again and down the stairs we went.

Robyn turned the television on as she passed by it then walked over to the couch. I was all set to watch whatever was on, anything to get this stiff roll of meat and grizzle down. I sat the glass down on the table and turned to watch what was on. "Bewitched" was on. I hated that show but I didn't care. My plan was to sit there for a few more minutes and think of some excuse to go, rush home and take matters into my own hands to prevent my testicles from exploding.

I sat there watching that stupid show for only a few minutes while Robyn was doing what sounded like straightening up the clutter from off the couch. After those few minutes, I turned from the T.V. to see what Robyn was doing as I could no longer hear her movements. After turning in her direction, I had to grab on to my jaw to keep it from hitting the floor.

At that moment, I had just realized that Robyn's odd look after standing from the couch wasn't one of "I can't believe you tried to take advantage of me." It was more of a look of, "let's take this downstairs because I can't have my dad finding ass prints on the plastic of this couch."

There, standing before me without an ounce of clothing on was the girl of the neighborhood with the woman's body. It looked better outside of the clothes too. Now, I'm not quite sure how I got naked, I think I blacked out for that moment and was on automatic pilot. The next thing I realized was being naked, between her legs and pumping like there was no tomorrow. I had finally accomplished my mission.

Robyn and I never quite became what you would call boyfriend and girlfriend. Instead, we would get together and sit outside on the porch and talk. We never even really hung out around the neighborhood either. I would usually walk up to her house or she would walk down to mine. Both of our parents began to expect to see us together and viewed our relationship as harmless. We were viewed by them as just two buddies sitting on the porch giggling. What they didn't know was that we were going at it like professional porn stars every chance that we got. I would go by her house most days and sit and chat for hours then head down the hill and hang out with my buddies. While visits to my house also seemed innocent, the truth of the matter is, the only time that Robyn would come down to my house was to remove her clothing and point her toes toward the ceiling.

Robyn and I carried on in this fashion for years. Throughout the years she had boyfriends and I had other girlfriends but we always, no matter what or who was in our lives, we would always get together for a good sweat and smile session. It wasn't until she left for college that I finally realized how much I really cared for her.

Michelle too, had left for school. She had been accepted into the University of Connecticut and was now a Freshman there. She wanted to be a lawyer. I knew that she was now on her way to marrying some law student or even a future doctor. So, I guess at that juncture of my life I realized that the chances of us ever truly being together again were very slim. Sadly, I piled all hopes of ever seeing my Michelle again in a large stack and used the pieces of my broken heart as kindling to be ignited by the flames of the still heated passion, lust, and love that I continued to have for her.

Chapter 5 - The Runner

Time was moving fast. It was my senior year in high school and my thirst was back. With Robyn gone along with the others that bored me, I decided to take a short sabbatical. I thought maybe it was time for me to stop all of this nonsense and finally get my mind together. After all, this was my last year of high school and college was right around the corner.

Weeks had passed. I could now sneeze and produce an erection without thought. Things had gotten pretty bad for me. I knew that I needed something to take my mind off of soft, naked flesh, you know, an outlet. I tried everything. I had given myself so many self-inflicted pleasures that my fingers had molded themselves in a curled position. I would wake up the next morning after a long session of pleasing myself looking like a G.I. Joe with the Kung Fu grip. I was yanking and tugging on this thing three to four times a day. And if it were true what they say about masturbation making you go blind, I was sure to soon be fitted for a pair of Ray Charles sunshades. I mean, I saw stars at times and everything even went completely dark a few times after my explosion but my vision would always return. That would give me a scare but once the fear meter lowered and the horny meter raised, I was back at it. Hell, I figured if I did go blind, I could whack off with the lights on because they would no longer be a distraction.

I kept contemplating over and over what I could possibly do to occupy the sex portion of my mind before I skinned myself alive. Suddenly, I found what I had been looking for. This would be my outlet. This could save me from cramped up fingers and dehydration. This could be my be all. This had everything that a good whacking had with one exception and there was no cleanup. This would rev up my heart, make me sweat and have me exhausted after I was done. I could do it alone or with others. I could do it whenever I wanted to and it wouldn't make me go blind. My mind was made up, that very next morning I went down to the school gym and I joined the track team.

That was just what I needed. I know, it doesn't make sense but there was a method to my madness. During school, I had asked my buddy Mike about walking down to the basketball court to hang out. That was where most of the kids from my neighborhood and other kids hung out, especially the girls. The guys would play ball and show off for the girls while the girls sat on the tables under the tree and talked about which boy they liked. I had decided that going after the ladies and doing what I liked so much was inevitable so why continue to fight it. But to my disappointment and yet to my good fortune, my salvation was placed before me. Mike couldn't make it to the court this particular day because he was staying after school to try out for the track team and suggested that I do the same. At first, I thought, *track? Who in the hell runs track?* And I responded to him in kind.

"Mike, who in the hell runs track? You can't get girls running no damn track!"

"Sure, you can, man there's plenty of chicks that come to track meets," he responded.

"Seriously, then how come you don't have a girlfriend Mr. Track Star?"

"Because I don't want one, they're nothing but trouble."

"Obviously you've never had any because you'd definitely see that sometimes it's worth dealing with a little trouble. Oh, there's definitely an upside to having a girlfriend man."

"See, that's exactly why you need to be running track!" Mike said.

"Why, because I like girls?"

"No, because you fool with so many of them and one of these days it's going to catch up to you. You're gonna get caught fooling around by another one or some jealous boyfriend and they're all gonna want to kill your ass, so maybe it's best that you're trained to get out of there fast!"

Mike and I laughed at his highly unlikely but possible prediction and with all of that, I did try out and made the track team that very day. I was actually pretty fast too. Even though I had to run in those scrotum-crushing gym shorts, I had still somehow impressed the hell out of the coach. I was placed on the relay team and beyond my beliefs, I actually enjoyed it. I was part of a team something that I was definitely not use to. There were only two boys on the entire team faster than myself but they too recognized my talent and quickly spread the news. It wasn't long before the entire school body knew of my potential stardom. I had it made. The track team had captured and held my attention, well at least up until about the fourth day. Prior to this day the temperature had been pretty cool and we worked out with our sweat pants on. On this particular day, the sun was warming the earth more than sufficiently. The guys and all of the girls that were also members of the team removed their thick cotton sweats and began to warm up. I couldn't help myself. I tried, really, I did. I was now surrounded by a sea of round plump asses. As I stood there watching the tight figured athletic girls run by, I realized that a baton was not the only stick that I wanted to pass on to one of them that day. I could begin to feel my testicles being pushed against by the two thick straps that were using every bit of resistance to secure the heated beast from pushing its way out of the jockey harness under my running shorts. It was hard. No, not my penis, it was hard trying to stay focused with all of those half naked, tight bodied girls running about. Well, yeah, my penis had gotten hard too but I'm sure that you already knew that. *No need to stop here to visualize that, just continue to read on.*

Weeks had passed and I still hadn't quite gotten used to sharing the same field with the young women of the team. I had somewhat adjusted though. I had somehow now managed to keep my heated urges hidden. Although extremely difficult, I concealed my lust. As time passed slowly, I was able to consume myself with my new-found sport. What started out as sexual therapy for me now had become a part of me. I found myself seriously training daily. I would run three to four miles daily, stretch for an hour and then worked out in the weight room. I realized that there was something besides chasing pleasure that I was actually good at. It had become my new passion and I wanted to compete. I wanted to prove to myself that I was as good as I felt that I was. This was something that I was soon to find out as we had our first track meet on the upcoming Saturday at Hayfield High School.

Excited and pumped up, the members of the team along with the coaches lined up toward the exits of the bus wearing our school colored warm-up suits of blue and gold. One by one we piled off of the bus and headed for the already crowded field for preparation. We stretched and trotted around the field getting our muscles warm and limber. I was ready. I ran the one-hundred-yard dash and was the anchor man of the relay team which comprised of four of the fastest guys on the track team. We were pumped up about the meet and knew we were ready for any team out there.

Several events had started around the track area. The long jump, the javelin throw, and the shot-put events had gotten underway. Finally, what I had been waiting for, the relay team events were about to start. We all got into position. Derrick was our starter and could move like the wind. I knew that if he could get us started, that would be the end of the race because there would be no catching us from there.

The runners took their marks and got set into their starting positions. The loud sound of the pistol rang out and off they went. Derrick started out like a locomotive, gaining inches with each long stride. He had taken the lead quickly by a substantial margin. As he approached Jose, I watched as he started his trot away from Derrick. Derrick was now behind Jose. Without looking back, Jose reached behind as Derrick stretched his arm forward and placed the baton into the hand of his teammate. Jose took off. His legs were moving quickly almost as if they had a mind of their own. Unlike the smooth graceful strides of Derrick, Jose ran clumsy. It definitely wasn't poetry in motion but he was fast.

Jose had now secured the lead by an even wider span. He approached Reginald and passed him the baton and he quickly made his way around the short portion of track. He too, held on to the lead. I was ready. As he approached, I started running away from him. He neared and my arm extended backward toward him. I felt the baton touch my palm and I closed my grip. The sound of the baton hitting the ground caught my attention and I had suddenly realized that the small metal stick was not in my possession. I could hear my teammates screaming "Pick it up! Get it, quick!" I turned and rushed over to pick up the baton and turned. In just that short time, two of the runners from the other schools had blew by me. I ran as fast as I could. I would love to tell you that that I ran so fast that I passed them both and crossed the finish line and won first place but that what be a huge lie. Instead, we got fourth. I felt terrible. We lost our very first relay race because of my mistake. I knew that I had to shake this feeling because I still had the one-hundred-yard dash to compete in and I was planning to make up for my mistake. No one, not even the coach came over to say, "That's alright, we'll get 'em next time" or "Hey, everybody makes mistakes" nothing! No one but Carla. Carla walked up to me and said, "Don't worry about it, the same thing has happened to me, not once but twice. You still have another event and I know you can win. Besides, as a little incentive if you win, I'll give you anything you want."

I looked at her trying to conceal the solemn expression that rested on my face. After realizing what her proposal entailed, I lowered my head once again but this time only to peer at the two round melons protruding from her tight-fitting track jersey. I slowly raised my head and produced a huge smile. She stepped closer to me and glanced around before placing her hand gently on my jockstrap then licked her lips. As she walked away I stared at the crease lines of where her thighs and buttocks met at the bottom edge of her running shorts. It took everything that I could muster up to keep my composure.

The event was called and I rushed over to take my position for the one-hundred-yard dash. I was warm and ready to prove to myself and the coach that there was no one out there that I couldn't outrun. And since Carla had fueled my proton pack with desire, Superman himself wouldn't have been able to beat me that day.

The starter yelled out, "Runners take your marks… get set…" Just then the image of Carla's nice backside and legs popped into my mind. I was now visualizing me laying between her legs giving it to her and of course, my temperature down there began to rise. The pistol exploded and so did I. I was burning down the track like fire. I was on a mission and Carla was it. The faster I ran the harder I got until suddenly, my hard erection pulled my jockey strap over. It pinched the side of left testicle causing me excruciating pain. But even in agony, I continued burning down that track like a 1957 Chevy. The only problem was, the other runners must have been moving like the wind because they blew my fire out as they swished by me in a blur. I came in dead last with my protruding boner crossing the finish line before I did.

The ride back to school was brutal. I could hear the faint whispers and chuckles throughout the bus. I was tagged as the clumsy, skin baton anchor of the team. They laughed as they said that my pecker was faster than I was. I knew I would become the laughing stock of the school come that Monday. My outlet didn't seem much like an outlet or therapy any more. My track career had ended as quickly as it had begun. I continued to go to practice every evening only to talk to the girls that I so desperately wanted to get next to but nothing ever transpired. I guess my fast pecker didn't even impress them. Carla never spoke to me again after that day but would giggle along with her girlfriends every time she would walk by me in the hallway. My life, reputation and any chance of getting laid with ANY girl in school was over. So, it was back to my dark bedroom and to the only two ladies that understood me. The women that cared for me no matter what. My two favorite girls, Jergen's Lotion and Rosie Palm.

Chapter 6 - Satisfaction "101"

It was in October when my real schooling had begun. This was the month that my dad's play sister came to live with us. Her name was Sandra. Sandra was about four years younger than my dad and had grown up just down the street from him just outside of Dallas. Their mothers were the best of friends just as Sandra and my dad were, so much that they referred to each other as brother and sister. Sandra had just moved up from the Dallas area and needed a place to stay until she could find an apartment. She had accepted a nursing position here prior to her relocation and wanted to start right away. My mother loved Sandra dearly as well and welcomed the idea of her moving in with us.

Sandra was a beautiful woman. Her long dark curly hair caught the attention of both men and women alike. My mom always complimented her on her pretty olive complexion and told her to be careful up here in the city because the men here would go crazy over a pretty face like hers. As for myself, I thought it was the shapely legs and that nice ass that she was totin' around that the men would probably be chasin' after buy hey, that's just me.

Months had passed quickly and Sandra continued with the same routine that she had originally started just after her arrival. She would get up, go to work, come home, eat, shower then watch television before going to bed. She didn't date, socialize or even go out to the movies, so the chances of her meeting a man was very slim, well at least I thought so.

It wasn't until the day of my mom's birthday that Sandra had graced the family with a date of her own. Harvey was his name. He was a large man in stature and appeared to be very boisterous. His personality in my mind just didn't go with that of Sandra's. She seemed a lot more conservative than he but I guess it's true what they say, "Opposites attract."

For her birthday, my dad had taken my mother to dinner and to a show that night and had asked Harvey and Sandra to accompany them. Since I wasn't invited, I gathered my things and headed down the hill to meet up with the guys. I had been hanging out for a few hours before deciding to head back home to grab a bite to eat. I usually stayed out until late but knowing that my parents and Sandra were out, I could practically have the house to myself and you know what that means. I figured a quick bite followed by me relieving myself made for a good night.

As I approached the house, I could see Harvey's big shiny Cadillac resting in the parking space that it had occupied earlier. I was actually surprised that they didn't take his car to the theater since it was much larger than my dad's Chevy Nova. *"I wonder if he left his keys too,"* I thought as I climbed the stairs quickly. I entered the house and headed over to the empty fruit bowl where my mom and dad normally kept their keys but to my dismay, it was empty. After the thought of going for a quick joy ride had vacated my crazy mind I headed straight for the refrigerator. I was starving and since I wasn't invited to dinner with the grownups I had to fend for myself. I pulled the loaf of bread from the breadbox, made a peanut butter and jelly sandwich then poured myself a large glass of milk. The house was peaceful and quiet. Not even the sound of Sandra's television set that was always on interrupted my meal. Nor was she sitting in the living room with my dad as they always did. I sat my meal on the dining room table then walked over and opened the back door to see if anyone was outside. The neighborhood too, was quiet and vacant. I gently pushed the door shut, returned to the dining room and began to devour my meal. All was calm and quiet during that moment. I chucked the last corner of my sandwich into my mouth and grabbed my cold glass of milk which was now half full. As I raised the glass to my mouth, I heard something. Since I wasn't sure if it was coming from inside the house, I stilled myself. I sat quietly and motionless. I listened. The sound was faint and muffled but was now beginning to increase in volume. As the sound intensified, so did my curiosity. I quietly pushed myself up from the table and tiptoed toward the front door. The sound appeared to be coming from outside. I eased over to the front door and stood. I slowly leaned over and pressed my ear against the door and listened. The muffled sound was no longer present. Now figuring that it was probably a car or maybe a passerby, I turned to head back toward the kitchen. Then suddenly, just as quickly as it had dissipated, the muffled sound returned. I froze in my tracks. Not moving an inch, I just stood and listened. It was then that I realized that the constant, faint sound wasn't coming from outside, it was coming from upstairs. It was the sound of moaning, Sandra's moans.

Not sure what was going on, I quietly made my way up the stairs then cautiously down the hall to her room. As I neared the room, I could see that the door was shut but I could still hear the moaning and panting. My first thought was that she heard the back door shut and thought that I had gone back outside and resumed a good masturbation session that I had interrupted. I then wondered if she was ill or in some type of pain.

The moans continued to escape from behind the closed door and became more intense as did my interest. I soon ruled out the illness theory because the moans and pants began to sound like the moans and pants coming from my bedroom during my alone time. These were definitely moans of pleasure. This changed everything. I couldn't help my perverted self. I had to see. I just had to see what she was doing to herself. *"Was she naked?"* I wondered. *"That would make a nice visual aide during my next session,"* I thought. After standing there for a moment picturing Sandra naked and holding my crotch, my mind returned to the closed door. Knowing that I wouldn't be able to live with myself if I hadn't looked inside that room, I gripped onto the knob of the door. As the cold bead of sweat slowly slid down my temple, I very slowly turned the doorknob. I pushed ever so slightly then paused for a second hoping she didn't see me. I slid my left eye through the small opening and inhaled an eye full. I had never been so wrong. There was no masturbation going on at all. With my eye pressed through the cracked opening and my mouth wide open, I peered inside the room in amazement. There, straddling a man that we had all just met was dad's play little sister.

With a deep arch in her back, she revved back just prior to thrusting herself forward against the man's pelvic area. She moaned in ecstasy as he gripped on to her buttocks and met her powerful thrust halfway with an equally powerful impale of his own. I became immersed in the sensual act of the two and continued to watch for several minutes, mainly focusing on her perfect, beautiful round bottom. She began to thrust faster and with more force while he continued to match her thrust for thrust. Suddenly, I heard him scream out, "Oh damn!" I watched on as his legs trembled and twitched. He now gripped even tighter to her lovely ass. My eyes made their way up her perspiration covered back then up to her sensual shoulders and finally into her dark beautiful eyes. That's right, her eyes. After pleasuring him she looked back toward the door and peered directly into my eye that was now protruding through the opened seam of the doorway then in a seductive manner, she only smiled.

"How long had she known that I was there?" I thought. She made her dismount from the man and headed over in my direction. Instead of waiting around to see what she would say, I made a quick

departure downstairs, through the kitchen then out the back door. As I hurried out through the back gate, I looked up at the bathroom window and there, standing, peering at me from the window was Sandra.

Things were different between Sandra and me after that incident. The following day I tried avoiding her. I had no idea what to say. Actually, I was a little embarrassed. The only thing that I did know was that I had plenty of new masturbation material for my night life. She was hot! Every day that followed, I could barely make eye contact with her. I never told a soul what I had seen; I just played it back almost nightly in my mind.

Weeks had passed and I still avoided Sandra like the plague. She too, had continued on as if nothing had happened at all. It was a Friday night and my parents had suited up in their night garb and were heading down the stairs as I entered the front door.

"Alright sport, hold down the fort. Your mom and I will be back in a little while," My dad said cheerfully.

"Yeah, there're some chops and mashed potatoes on top of the stove. You may have to heat them up but there's plenty," My mom said in a bubbly tone.

I nodded then asked what I always did, "Where are you guys headed?"

And as always, they both looked back at me and spoke as if rehearsed, "OUT!" they both yelled simultaneously then rushed out the door. I shut the door then headed for the kitchen to attend to those chops that my mom had mentioned.

I popped the plate of fried meat into the microwave to nuke them to a temperature more suitable for my meal. I pulled a plate from the cabinet above the sink and two slices of bread from the unsealed bag and made a sandwich. I walked out onto the front porch and began to devour my white meat sandwich as if it were the first meal that I had had in weeks. As I sat there, I happened to notice Sandra's car parked across the street from the house. I wasn't even aware that she was home.

I knew I didn't want to be there alone the house with her. It would have been her opportunity to confront me about that night and I didn't want that, not at all. I quickly rose from my resting place and hurried into the kitchen. I slid the remaining portion of my sandwich onto a paper towel and headed for the door. I wanted to grab some of my music from my bedroom to take with me to my buddy's house but decided not to risk running into her. That's when I heard it. Just as I had reached the front door, I heard the bathroom door shut just prior to the shower being turned on. After a brief moment, I could hear the shower curtain being flung open. The sound of the running water grew louder then quickly became muffled as the curtain was pulled shut. No more than a few seconds later the humming of an old gospel hymn rang out from the perfect acoustics of the bathroom walls. That was it. That was my opportunity to quickly sneak upstairs, grab my music from my room and ease out the door undetected. My plan was simple.

I inched slowly up the stairs. I could hear the water running clearly now. I tipped back to my room and over to the old record player sitting on the small table near my bedroom window. I rummaged through the stack of albums gathering only those that I wanted to take with me. I placed the album jackets under my arm then turned to make my quiet exit and that's when I saw the small neatly folded piece of paper stuffed under the wooden jewelry box on top of my dresser. I stopped and pulled it out from its concealed area and unfolded it. It was a note from Sandra. It read: *I am so sorry about the other night. I didn't mean for you to see that and both your mother and father would be really upset with me if they knew about this. They would also be upset to find out that you stood there and spied on me the way you did too. How about we keep this our little secret?*
Sandra

I stood there with my mouth wide open. I understood exactly what she was saying. My "Peeping Tom" act was her leverage. I didn't care though. Just knowing that she felt just as guilty as I did, lifted a heavy weight from my shoulders. I re-folded the paper, slid it in my drawer and stood there for a second smiling to myself. I was no longer feeling guilty and suddenly realized that I also had her by the short and curlys just as she did me.

As I turned to exit my room, the door to the bathroom opened suddenly. I had gotten so caught up with the letter I hadn't even noticed that the thunderous sound of the rushing water from the shower had now ceased. Now, standing before me was the woman that I had been making love to in my palm for the past several weeks. Standing there smiling wearing only a towel. Once again, my mouth had fallen wide open and without any assistance from my mind, my voice spoke, "Oh, my God, just once!"

The words had left my mouth before my mind had a chance to process, filter, and redeliver. Yep, it came out in raw form. She walked up to me then slowly turned and stepped inside her room. Before closing her door, she spoke out in a calm, seductive voice, "Don't write a check with your mouth that your ass can't cash. What you need to do is behave yourself, with your mannish self."

Like some of you, I too didn't know what in the hell that meant. It took me a second to figure it out. I mean, who writes a check with their ass? Hell, I didn't even have a damn checking account. Anyway, by the time I figured it out, the door was shut.

As I walked by her door, I mumbled just loud enough for her to hear, "Humph, if I write a check, you'll know your butt has been paid, that's for sure!" then headed for the stairs. After just making it down only three steps, Sandra's door re-opened. I stopped and awaited her snide reply. Her response was a lot more dynamic than I had expected. She merely stood there quietly, dropped her towel, slowly pushed her door opened then walked back into her room and over to her bed. And like any other horny idiot, I stood there frozen.

After collecting myself, I realized that this was probably a once in a lifetime opportunity. This was an invite. Well in my mind it was an invite. For her, it could have been a challenge or punishment for me after talking so much trash. After giving it little to no thought, I quickly spun around and returned up the stairs and into her room. Actually, I don't even recall walking back up the steps. Hell, I don't even remember walking at all. As I entered her bedroom I thought of something suave to say that would perhaps make her look at me as a more mature guy but that didn't work either. As she lay there completely naked on her bed I was speechless. If you had asked me my name at that moment, I wouldn't have been able to tell you. I couldn't utter one vowel or sound out one letter. I tried to speak but gave up. I remember visualizing that stupid chart with the pictures on it, hoping that method would assist me with speaking. I remember thinking, *pig...pu, wheel...wu, fan... fu, top...tu . Oh, to hell with it!*

Finally, my brain restarted. I looked down at her as she lay there rubbing lotion on that wonderful body of hers. After inching just a little closer, I cleared my throat then added as much bass as I could muster up.

"Here, let me get that for you," I said trying while trying to keep my composure.

She passed me the bottle of lotion and I placed my finger over the pump and held out my hand to catch the cold, skin lubricant. Before I had a chance to push down on the dispenser Sandra slid down on the bed and spread her legs wide and once again smiled at me. Now, I'm sure that I don't really have to tell you this but, I had so much blood rushing to the center of my body that I got light headed.

The lotion shot across the room and I felt as though I could have too. I dropped the bottle on the floor and began removing my shirt. She rolled over on her side and began assisting me with my pants. I couldn't believe what was about to happen. My pants dropped to the floor quickly followed by my underwear. I stepped out from them after removing my shoes which had kept me captive. I reached for my socks but she stopped me. She pushed me back and just stared at me shockingly. I could tell from the surprised expression on her face that she was both shocked and impressed with what I had to offer. I gripped on to my throbbing manhood and climbed aboard. I was ready to unleash the hounds of hell into her awaiting pool of fire but she interrupted me once again. She placed her hands of the side of my hips and prevented me from entering her. She looked up at me and gently said, "If you tell anybody about this, anybody at all, this will be your first and last time in here."

I looked down at her shaking my head franticly, "I won't, I won't tell anybody, I promise."

She removed her hands from my thrusters and like a rocket I was insider her. I was pumping like I was out to win the Guinness Book of World Records in stroking. I couldn't believe that I was actually doing this. This had just become the best day of my life. She felt so good. Actually, she felt too good because I could already feel the electricity of my orgasm building. As an experienced woman, she too could sense that I was about to blow a little too soon for her liking. I was out of control but somehow, she managed to take control. Once again, she placed the palms of her hands against my pumping hips. I stopped for a moment as she spoke gently and calmly to me, "Slow down baby, we've got plenty of time. It ain't going nowhere."

With that, I did just that, I slowed down. My pelvic thrust transformed into smooth slow slides which she seemed to enjoy. I too had begun to get great pleasure out of the slow stroke. I had regrouped and pushed into her slowly where I was reciprocated by a returned grind from her. Suddenly without warning, she rolled me over and mounted me. She rode me like an old stallion. Her thrusts were hard, slow and steady picking up in pace as her excitement grew. She was now bearing down on me, forcing me deeper inside her with each thrust. I began to grit my teeth together as I concentrated on holding on to my fluids. She was bucking harder now and I was starting to feel the electricity begin to build again. Suddenly, she screamed out and gripped firmly onto her breast. "Oh shit!" she yelled.

Her stroke slowed until it ceased and she looked down upon me with a look of such satisfaction and gratitude that I was almost tempted to shake her hand. With her body now limp, she slowly made her dismount. *Uh, what about me?* I thought. I should have known, with all of her experience, she definitely knew how to satisfy a man and she wasn't done. She lowered herself between my legs and rested her elbows on the outside of my thighs. She slowly lowered her mouth on me. Her tongue was like a warm piece of silk that was being guided over me. It touched areas that had never been explored by anyone else, not even me. Finally, after the tongue expedition, she slid me inside her mouth. *Good Gugga Mugga!* Never in my life had I experienced a sensation even close to this. She continued for several minutes before hitting me with the grand finally. Sandra placed my member inside her hand. While sliding her hand gently up and down the shaft of my stiff penis, she continued to roll her tongue around its head until I could take no more. I blew like a 1965 ten cent can of shaken Coca Cola. I came so hard that I could have sworn that I could feel my socks shoot right off of my feet. I instantly fell in love with Sandra. *Well yeah, it was lust but I didn't know that then so I'm sticking to the love thing for now.*

Sandra and I continued having what we referred to as "Tutoring" sessions every chance that we got. It was just that too, tutoring. I was taking "Satisfaction 101" and Professor Sandra was giving me plenty of lectures and homework. I was learning something new every time we connected, sometimes even things that I didn't want to learn.   I remember the first time that she pushed my head down there. I looked at her with a blank look on my face as if to ask, "What? *Just what in the hell do you want me to do down here?*" Aware of what I was thinking, without any hesitation the Professor answered my question using only two words... "Lick it."

Now come on folks, we're talking about a seventeen-year-old in the 1970's. You know the saying back then, "If it ain't fried, I don't eat it!"

I looked Sandra in the eyes and realized that if I did that and word got out, I could never be able to show my face in the neighborhood again. There was no reason for me to do everything that she wanted me to. After all, she was getting pleasure out of this just like I was. I had made up my mind. I looked at Sandra as I hoisted myself up on my elbows and said as sternly as I could... "You're not going to tell anybody if I do, will you?"

Sandra smiled at me and without answering my question; she simply placed her hand back on top of my head and gently pushed it back between her legs. As I did as she had requested, she continued to coach me in that area of her pleasure too. As weeks passed, I became very proficient in pleasuring her in this way. This led to a shift in our relationship. She became the aggressor and I gave it to her when I wanted to which was still all the time but I like to think that I had the upper hand at this point. Sometimes that's all we did. She would satisfy me orally then I would return the gesture, sometimes even when my mom was asleep. We would sneak down the basement, the living room or anywhere else that we thought we could get away with it. When we were alone, those were the best times. We would pleasure each other then lie there and talk for hours. She would tell me about her job and her goals and sometimes about her past relationships. I would tell her about Michelle. We had gotten out of hand but as they say, God looks out for babies and fools because we were surely acting foolish. I would have been beaten within an inch of my life if I had ever gotten caught and Sandra, well let's just say, they probably would have never found the body.

It wasn't until I was informed of Sandra's moving that we shared our first kiss. Somehow, I think we both felt that if we didn't kiss it made things seem like it wasn't so wrong. I know, here we are screwing around two and three times a day but a kiss somehow made us virgins. *I don't know, I was young and getting laid, you make it make sense.*

Anyway, she knew how much I cared for her but she knew it was time to move forward with her life. She now had more than enough money to get on her feet. My parents would have probably let her stay forever, which would have been just fine with me but she wasn't the type, she needed her own. When I asked her to stay, she only looked at me and smiled. Taking me gently by the side of the face with both hands she pressed her lips against mine softly before slowly sliding her tongue into my mouth. It was so special but for some reason, that moment made me think of Michelle.

Sandra eventually did move. I walked around moping for weeks. My mother asked me several times what was wrong but of course I could never tell her about what Sandra and I had.

Chapter 7 - Fly Boy

With the summer now over and the best sex that I ever had and thought that I ever would have gone, I was back in school and now in my senior year. The school year had breezed by in the blink of an eye. Before I realized it, graduation was here. I still thought of Sandra often and Michelle still even more but they were both gone. I still had sex with them both as often as I could and must have gone through a box of tissue a week and lotion even faster. I had them on my mind so much I had hardly given graduation, prom or my life after high school any thought whatsoever. I knew my time was running out because if there's one thing that my dad stressed; independence. He'd say, "Son, after you graduate high school you've got four choices; college, the military, work and pay rent here or live on your own." He made it clear that I would not be living at home rent free after high school.

I knew he meant that too. It was time for me to figure out my future. I began contemplating my options, "*If only there was some type of job in the sex field I could get without getting killed by my parents,*" I thought. I stood there chuckling for a moment then quickly returned my focus to the serious matter at hand. Work sounded good, you know, making my own money and all but without any real experience, what could I do, what would I become? I knew some of the guys were going off to college but more school just didn't appeal to me very much. More studying, more books and more lectures that would take everything that I have just to stay awake, no, school is not for this guy. My decision had been made. I decided to look for a job, stay home and pay rent and maybe see Sandra occasionally. That sounded like my best recourse. That Friday, I headed downtown and applied for employment at every department store, bank and even at the city newspaper. I stopped by the grocery store and the neighborhood dry cleaners and applied there as well. I was sure to have a job lined up before graduation.

Weeks had passed and I received no response from any of the places where I had applied. I couldn't believe it. Who wouldn't want to employ a willing young man of my stature? I was beginning to panic because I knew that I was running out of time. I also knew that one week after my graduation, dad would be expecting me to be heading out for work the same as he did every day or packing my belongings. My mother would probably try to convince him to give me an extension but I knew my dad, no chance.

The day of my graduation was great. I strolled across the stage with my chest protruding and swollen with pride as I received my diploma. My family cheered as I was handed the roll of paper and shook the hand of the principle. Everyone was there and I felt so important. After the ceremony had come to a close, everyone gathered in front of the school where I receive more congratulatory offerings and stood for the special day photos. After all of the picture taking was finished, the group of family and friends departed. Most of my relatives gathered at the house where we had a great feast. It was so much fun. Everyone gave me gifts and cards containing money. After the last of the guest swung the gate shut I sat in solitude on the back porch inhaling the remains of the day. The squeaking from the rusty screened door opening interrupted my thoughts. I exhaled then looked over my shoulder. It was my dad. He walked down to the second step and sat down next to me. He held two iced cold beers in his hands. He raised one up and over in my direction then smiled. *"This is a first,"* I thought. I mean, as a younger kid he'd give me a sip or two from his can but to offer me a whole beer made me feel like a man. I didn't react at first then he pushed it closer. "Beer son, you deserve it?" he asked.

"Uh… yeah, sure," I replied smiling.

He popped the tops off of the cans and passed me one. I took two huge gulps from the can quickly thinking I'd better get as much as I could before he changed his mind. He took a sip from his can then tapped me on the knee.

"Great party, wasn't it? Did you see how fat your cousin Jackie has gotten?"

"That wasn't Jackie, that was the lady that ate my cousin Jackie!" I said.

My dad acknowledged my comment with just a lowering of his head then turned to me and mumbled, "Now you know you ought to be ashamed of yourself for that, that's family you're talking about." After which, he turned to me with a strange gaze. He tried to contain it but couldn't. Moments after, we both broke into laughter and sipped our beers. "Yep, she surely has grown!" he said while chuckling.

We continued to laugh and discuss other members of the family and friends that came out to congratulate me. I should have seen it coming but it was too late. Things were going too good. After taking a huge gulp from his can, my dad placed his hand on my leg and looked me in the eyes. "So now that you've graduated what's next?"

"I don't know Dad. I mean, I really don't want to go to college but I do want to do something with my life. I did go and apply for some jobs downtown last weekend but haven't heard anything yet."

"Yeah, it's hard finding your first job son. Have you tried the grocery stores?" he asked as he brushed the lint from his trousers.

"Yeah but I just can't see myself working at a grocery store pushing boxes."

"There's nothing wrong with that! You'll be making money and you'll be able to pay your bills."

"Dad, right now I don't have any bills."

He looked over at me and placed his hand on my shoulder smiling an odd kind of smile. "You do now son. Rent is due on the first of every month. I'll give you one month to find a job and if you don't you'll have to find someone else to stay with and freeload off of. You're a man now son and with manhood comes responsibility."

He stood up, looked down at me and returned into the house. I remained on the stoop sipping my "Man" can of beer while trying to determine my fate and I must say... it wasn't looking very promising.

The tapping of heels against the pavement reminded me of a room filled with typist pecking away on an old Remington typewriter. Downtown was as busy as usual even more so than on the weekend. I caught the bus down first thing in the morning. The busy streets were filled with buses, cars and the sidewalks were filled with working folk rushing to their offices to make their living like I so desperately needed to do. I applied for work at every mailroom, stockroom, and parking lot of every office building downtown. I re-applied at some of the same department stores that I had applied to just weeks before. No one gave me a warm and fuzzy feeling about hiring me. They all just nonchalantly took my application and brushed me off then quickly returned to the shadows of their offices.

As I once again headed for the bus stop with my tail between my legs I could hear his husky voice in the distance. "Young man, young man!"

Thinking it could be one of the managers from where I had applied, I turned quickly displaying a huge smile. There standing waving me over to him was a man standing in front of an opened door. He stood erect holding nothing but a folder. His uniform was neatly pressed with creases on each pant leg appearing as if they could cut you like a knife. His blue jacket was covered with medals and ribbons across the chest and you could see the reflection of your face off of his high gloss Corfam dress shoes. He was an Air Force recruiter. As soon as I was in listening distance he started in on me. He gave me the spiel about how hard it was to find a job these days and how "Uncle Sam" would take care of me. I guess I didn't appear too enthused so he continued hawking. It didn't much matter though because in my mind, the thought of even the mere possibly of going to war or getting shot at for whatever reason was less than appealing to me. I started to turn and walk away but for some strange reason I continued to listen. He spoke the same gibbly garb that I expected him to. You know, about how great the Air Force was and how I could see the world and get a college degree while I was in the military and of course how I would be doing my country a great service and all of that crap. When in fact, the only thing that he was trying to do was make his enlistment quota. He continued on nonstop. In my mind it was time to walk away. Now I was only hearing gibberish and still uninterested. Then suddenly he spoke those golden words that quickly caught my attention; "Plus the Air Force will give you a fifteen-thousand-dollar enlistment bonus." Fifteen thousand dollars! Now this was the first time that something outside of a female's body part was starting to give me a woody! He may as well have said one million gazillion billion dollars because to an eighteen-year-old, they're one and the same. I remember thinking, *where in the hell do I sign up?*

I returned home that day feeling proud and a little conned. I didn't find out until after I signed up that the fifteen thousand dollar carrot that he dangled in my face was to be rationed and dispensed to me over my enlistment term, six years. But even with that I still felt pretty good about the deal because I knew my family would be proud of the decision that I had made. My father would be especially proud because he too was ex-Air Force.

I was home for six weeks after graduation before I left for basic training. Yep, there was another party and Anita who I've always wanted, finally gave in and slept with me. I had wanted some of that since I was in the ninth grade but she just wouldn't give it up. I don't know what got into her. Maybe she thought she would never see me again or maybe she wanted to be the wife of an airman. I don't know but it didn't matter because after waiting that long and finally getting it, my only thought was *damn I waited this long for this…wasn't worth a damn!* After all that damn waiting, she laid there motionless the entire time with only an occasional grunt or sigh. Well I guess the sporadic murmurs did let me know that she was still alive at lease. I could've gotten more pleasure out of greasing up a hole in a stump! And she definitely couldn't compete with my hand.

After a while, I was so bored with Anita's comatose ass I just started practicing different types of strokes for the real deal. And can you believe it, she actually had an orgasm. Still, her body never moved during the entire orgasm. If it wasn't for the long deep grunt that she produced and the flooding of her insides I would have never known. Her left hand twitched for a minute and her eyes rolled to the back of her head. After that the session was over. Seems she was a "one hitter quitter." After her orgasm, her little kitty had become too sensitive and with every stroke after, she jumped, twitched or squirmed. Just when I was beginning to think that this could finally turn into a good ride, it ended. I pushed into her and she shot back slamming the back of her head into the headboard. Her head hit the solid structure so abruptly that I was sure that the collision had dazed her for a second. It became evident that she was fine as she placed her hands on both sides of my hips to impede my thrust. She looked at me in a sort of embarrassed way and said, "I can't take anymore. It's too sensitive right now." With that, I rolled off of her and got dressed. She asked me if I was upset and of course I lied and said no. After we parted ways, I found the satisfaction that I needed in the palm of my hand and of course, Michelle was my inspiration.

It was one of the hottest months of the year and I was heading down to one of the most sweltering cities in one of the most sweltering states in the country, San Antonio, Texas. That's where I spent several of the longest weeks of my life. I'll never forget climbing down off of that bus in the middle of the night to the loud yelling voices of the drill instructors.

"Get the hell off my bus, boy and get your filthy ass in line!" he shouted.

I realized at that particular moment I wasn't to expect Dorothy or Toto or anybody else from Oz to come wake me up from that bad dream. We scurried around like lost children in desperate need of guidance for the first few weeks and was taught everything from A to Z. We were taught survival techniques, how to shoot M16's, handguns and even how to fold our underwear. I didn't quite get that whole concept though. I mean let's be real here for a moment, if I was ever in a combat situation with bullets blazing and bombs or grenades exploding anywhere near me, every inch of the same underwear that I was to respect so much would be soiled anyway so why fold them?

Basic training really taught me a lot of things about honor, respect and self-control. Yep, it taught me that there was no honor in volunteering for anything. When we first arrived at boot camp that was one of the first lessons given. I remember our drill sergeant walking up to us in formation smiling. He looked around and once again smiled at us as if we all were good buddies just before asking a quite simple question, "How many good bowlers do we have in this fine group of men?"

We all looked around at each other wondering what he was getting at especially since he had just finished telling us that he would gladly rip off our heads and shit down our necks. So, it was only fitting for us to be just a little confused. But of course, you always have that first idiot. You know, the one that looks for the first easy way out of work. So yeah, I raised my hand, I was that idiot. I figured they must've had a bowling league on the base and needed members for the team. I couldn't bowl worth a damn but if it got me out of some of those lousy details, I was in.

After raising my hand, I was called to the front and soon followed by several other idiots like me who wanted to answer the call. We all stood there proudly, chests out and smiling. We were the new bowling team of Flight 186. The drill instructor stood before us with his hands on his hips then addressed each one of us independently asking what our bowling averages were. We shouted them out proudly and of course I lied and shouted out the same number as one of the other guys had shouted previously. He had us fall into formation and marched all nine of us toward the wide entranceway. As he turned to face us, his nice friendly smile dissipated.

"Alright maggots, there are exactly eighteen toilets in this latrine. Since you all are such great bowlers, each one of those bowls in there better be spit shined every night before lights out! That includes shitters, pissers and wash bowls. The floor will be clean enough to eat on so make sure it is because if it's not, every last one of you will be eatin' your breakfast on it the following mornin', got it?!" he commanded.

"Sir, yes Sir!" we all shouted in unison.

Ain't this a bitch, I thought. Here I was thinking I was doing something good, helping out, being patriotic or something and what did I get, the shaft. Well so much for honor and respect.

I did however learn a valuable lesson in self-control while there. It was truly an eye opener. After I had signed up and even after I had arrived for basic training, I hadn't realized one very important thing until I lay still in my bunk that very first night... there would be no sex for weeks, not even with myself. I couldn't breathe, my heart began to pound heavily and perspiration flowed down the side of my face. I was having a panic attack. I must have also suffered a mild case of temporary insanity as well because I could have sworn I heard my pecker speak clearly to me. I could feel it slithering out of the slot of my military issued skivvies, poking its head out and pointing at me. Then I saw the opening begin to move as if they were lips. That's when I heard it. I actually heard it speak to me. It was a faint whisper but clear enough for me to hear. As it spoke, I leaned my head forward to hear. I then heard it clearly say, "Bobby.... Bobby... you're a dumb ass Bobby. How could you do this to me... to us?" After this, it lay there motionless just staring at me then slowly slithered back inside my underwear. I believe I could hear it whimpering later that night but I left him alone and just gave him his space. I felt as if I had let him down. Suddenly I felt as if a huge blanket of depression had covered me. I also knew that from that moment on, I was going to do everything in my power to keep my mind off of tits and ass for the remaining weeks of my training.

It wasn't 'til the second week that we met our team leader and wouldn't you know it, our team leader was a woman. She was over the drill instructors assigned to our flight. I guess she would be considered their supervisor. I wasn't really worried though because this woman put the capital "U" in ugly. She looked like the love child of Donald Trump and Phyllis Diller. Her reddish-orange colored hair made her stand out when that was the last thing that she should have ever wanted. She had the biggest teeth that I had ever seen. When she spoke, she always made me think of Mr. Ed the talking horse. I wanted to ask her so bad to say just once, "Heeey Willlllllbeeeer!" but knew I'd only be thrown on restriction or worse. Now her body was definitely a conversation piece for us airmen. The shallow bulges that protruded from inside her blouse were either two flat fried eggs or the next size up from "man breast" that a woman could have. The long extension of her back that I guess she called an ass remained vacant. You could iron a shirt on that thing. And I don't want to even mention those sticks that were where her legs should've been. And to top everything off, the woman had the nastiest disposition that you would ever want to come across. She was the meanest person that I had ever met... she must've known she was ugly.

Here we were two weeks into basic training and just finding out that she would be the only female contact that we would see for weeks. Every night we would make cracks about Sergeant Sullivan.

"I wouldn't stick her with your dick," one airman would yell from his bunk.

"I would, if you replaced her head with Jayne Kennedy's and her body and legs with Lola Falana's. Hell, the only thing she could keep is her name," another airman would yell back.

This would go on for hours.

As the weeks progressed, so did we. We trained and trained and in the evenings, we would return to the barracks exhausted just after getting our daily chewing out from our beloved team leader, Sergeant Sullivan. The guys had weakened as had I and it was evident by the change in the nightly conversations. You wouldn't have never known that they were talking about the same woman that we had been introduced to just two weeks prior.

"Man, did you see those little sweet tits popping out from Sully's blouse today?" one of the airman asked out loud.

"Hell yeah, I would suck those things like I was dehydrated!" a response would be shouted back.

"And did you see that little tight ass pushing out of that skirt?" some other guy would ask.

These guys must have been delirious because I still saw the same ragamuffin that came to us two weeks ago. There was nothing about that woman that would make me stoop so low.

Two more weeks had passed and we were nearing the finish line. The drill instructors had let up on us somewhat and even "Evilina" herself had calmed down a bit. I was now even convinced that I was not delivered out of the womb of a dog since she had finally stopped calling us "Sons of bitches" fifty times a day. Most of the guys began to compliment her try to do things to stay in her good graces but in my eyes, she was still nothing but a skank in a blue uniform.

This particular morning the entire flight along with all of the other flights were assembled down on the parade grounds for graduation rehearsal. All but me of course. I was summoned do Sullivan's office. I had no idea why. After arriving, she asked me inside. She was looking extra ragged that morning. I was informed by her that with each graduation an airman is recognized for outstanding leadership and some other crap that I could care less about. I guess I should have looked at it as an honor to be considered for the award but instead I thought of my dad. I figured it would be something that would make my dad proud so what the hell. After she had made the announcement she continued complimenting me on what a model airman I was and how the other guys grew to respect me. She went on and on until I realized or my six-week horny ego lead me to believe that she was flirting with me. *Yuk! And hell no!* I thanked her and falsely complimented her on her fine work as a team leader, stood and asked for permission to leave. She stood up, walked around her desk and up to me. She gazed into my eyes for a moment, sighed deeply then stepped away. I thought, *"Damn, she must've had a fried shit sandwich for breakfast this morning anytime you can smell stank breath like that through her nostrils. And I know damn well she didn't think I would fall for that superiority gaze crap, it'll take more than that and ten million dollars to climb on top of her ugly ass."* Sullivan walked over and slammed her office door shut then returned over to me.

"Wouldn't you like to thank me for the recommendation?" she asked.

"Thank you," I replied while producing a nervous smile.

Sullivan placed her hand on my crotch and laid her head against my chest. I could still smell her breath, it smelled like zoo dust. Just like wild animals had been trampling around inside her mouth all night. She rubbed and stroked gently between my legs then spoke as seductive as she could. "Come on, you can do better than that, can't you?"

I stepped back out of range of that crop duster she called a mouth and walked away.

What, did you actually think that I was going to say that at that instant, I jammed my tongue into that garbage mouth and then made passionate love to her on the floor of her office as we gazed into each other's eyes? Oh, hell no! I stepped back from her ugly ass and walked right over to the door. I turned off the lights because there was no way that I was going to look at her ugly ass while getting my rocks off. And as to not smell her breath, I bent her over her desk and stroked her ugliness like there was no tomorrow. C'mon! you've been reading this book, what did you think my nasty ass was going to do, we're talking about me... Bobby.

After storing up these juices for all of those weeks and having an opportunity to release them, I took it. I bent her over that desk and heaved up her skirt. I reached down to slide her panties off but this evil, dusty whore in blue wasn't wearing any. I gleamed down at what appeared to be a board with a short vertical line drawn down the center before realizing it was her ass. I couldn't look long as I would have lost the erection that arrived with no assistance from me. Too impatient to slide my fatigues down, I pulled my throbbing flesh out through my zipper. I pushed inside her with no regard to wetness or tightness. I rammed in. As I began stroking this ugly critter, I was utterly surprised by how good it actually felt. She pressed her absent ass back against me with each thrust. I felt it.

"No, not yet," she moaned out.

I continued pumping.

"No, not yet damn it!" she yelled out.

"Ok, just let me..." It was too late. I must have set a new record. I haven't come that quick since I was twelve. I must've blown my wad in twenty strokes or less. Sullivan was pissed. I would have tried again but she turned around to scold me and I saw her and caught yet another whiff of that breath. I was done. As I was leaving her office she looked at me with that mean look that she had and said, "You can forget that recommendation, there's nothing outstanding about you, nothing at all! Now get your sorry ass outta my office."

I adjusted my clothes and walked out feeling lighter and happier for some reason. And for some reason, I gave no thought at all to the award or making my dad proud of me getting it. All I knew at that moment was... even at your lowest times... there's nothing like a good nut to make everything better. The sun looked brighter, I could now hear the birds chirping that I had never heard or seen before and the base took on an entire new look to me, it was beautiful. I actually felt like skipping.

I rushed down to the parade grounds, half running, half skipping but only to be met by my drill instructor Sergeant McEntire.

"Airman where in the hell have you been?" he asked.

"Sir, Sergeant Sullivan requested me in her office Sir!" I responded.

"Oh, so you were the pick of this class huh, so, how was she?"

"Sir?"

"How was she? The sex, how was it son?"

"Sir I..."

"Look airman, for every class, Sullivan picks one of the airman to do before they leave, you were it for this class. You fools fall for it every time. You boys have no self-control and it only tells you one thing about yourself son. It tells you that after only a few weeks restricted from women or some kind of self-inflicted sexual release... you'd fuck a dog."

The sergeant turned and walked off shaking his head. Now ashamed but still feeling lighter and relieved, I lowered my head and hurried over to formation to join the others. The damn birds stopped chirping and reality had quickly set back in, damn.

The last week had passed and graduation was finally at hand. We were finally leaving this God forsaken place and I was heading home for a week then off to my technical training school. We climbed onto the bus to head to the airport. As the bus slowly pulled away from the front of the barracks, Sullivan stepped out onto the lawn. I peered at her then quickly turned away. She looked as revolting as ever. I slowly turned back and looked at her. There still with the same snarl on her face, she continued her glare. I decided to be the better person so I raised my hand while displaying the best smile that I could muster up and waived to her. Her snarl diminished. She too began to smile then slowly raised her hand and gave me the finger. The bus headed down the road and I was relieved and yet just a little nauseous. I couldn't stop thinking about what I had done with that river rat just days before. After giving even more thought to that gross but enjoyable act with that horrible little woman with the breath of ten dead men... I vomited in my own mouth.

That Thursday, I arrived at National Airport. No one was there to meet me, not a sole so I hailed a cab and quickly climbed inside. I gave the driver the address of my parents' home and he quickly drove off. As the car sped through the busy city I reminisced on my childhood there. As we drove by the swimming pool where I once worked during the summer, I remembered my first genital scare. While working there at the pool, I use to take my break and lay back on the first aid cot in the office to escape from the sun. I'll always remember that. For it was then that I learned my first lesson in pain and frustration. It was there where I caught the crabs. Those little sons of bitches nearly ate my balls off! I had no idea what they were or how they got there. I found out later that most of the supervisors were screwing around on that cot after hours. They must have been some nasty asses on that poor cot. Not wanting my mother to know, I had to sneak to the clinic to only face the embarrassment. I had to ointment down these nuts for weeks. Just thinking about it still gives me the willies! It was an ordeal that I could've done without.

After revisiting that memory, I no longer wanted to think. I laid my head back and closed my eyes until we arrived at my parents' home. After pulling up in front of the house, I climbed out of the cab and retrieved my duffle bag from the trunk of the car then quickly paid the driver. I walked up the stairs which led to the already opened door of the house and stepped inside. There she sat. "Hey Ma, how are you?" I said smiling at her.

She looked up at me and the biggest smile that I had ever seen lit up her beautiful face. She quickly hopped up from her seat chuckling.

"My Lord, look at you! A real military man and looking so handsome, wow! Your daddy and I thought that you were coming home on Saturday."

"Well yeah, I was going to hang around in San Antonio for a couple of days with some of the guys but decided to head on home instead. I have to report to Keesler Air Force Base on the 22nd."

"Well come on back in the kitchen because I know you're hungry. It's so good to see you," she said while pinching my cheek.

Mom, with her arms gripped tightly around my waste, guided me toward the kitchen where she continued to compliment my uniform and my newfound muscles. She updated me with all the neighborhood current events, with one almost stopping my heart. Having no idea of how important the news of the death of Michelle's mother was to me, my mother blurted it out as if she were discussing sales at the local grocery store.

"Oh yeah, you remember Mrs. Taylor? You know, the lady who lived next to the church house?" she said nonchalantly.

"Yeah, of course, you're talking about Michelle's mom, right?"

"Oh yeah, I forgot about Michelle. She's been away for so long but yeah, her mom. The poor woman died this past Sunday morning, heart attack I think is what they said it was."

"What! Died?"

"Yep. I stopped by and spoke with her brother just yesterday to see if they needed anything and sat with them for a while."

"Have they made the arrangements yet? Man, I'm so sorry to hear that. Michelle must be going crazy."

"You ought to stop by and at least give the family your condolences."

"Yeah, I'll stop by after I get cleaned up," I said still looking on in disbelief.

"Well come on in here, you'd better eat something first."

I sat down and had a nice meal of chicken, rice and gravy with my mother then rushed upstairs to shower and change. I had to go see how Michelle was. I wanted to let her know that I was here for her during this difficult time and to also find out how she was doing. You know, see if she was seeing anybody and more importantly, hoping to share some of my newly learned and now mastered skills with her.

After I was dressed, I headed for the back door.

"Take that apple pie I baked for the family," my mother shouted.

"Ok," I yelled from the kitchen.

I walked through the back door and down the alley with one of my mother's favorite pieces of glassware bearing a freshly baked pie. I turned up the hill, through the gate and was standing at the front door of the girl of my dreams just as I had done so many times before as a kid. I smiled to myself as I thought about those old appointments of ours. I knocked on the door softly then waited for a response.

The tall thin man opened the door slowly then stood there glaring at me momentarily. It was Sonny, Michelle's mom's brother. I remembered him well. As kids we all use to call him "Uncle Sonny." I remembered him spraying us almost every Saturday morning with water from the hose while washing his car. He would wash that old Pontiac of his every Saturday. He kept that car spotless and us along with it on those hot afternoons.

Sonny pulled the door toward him as he stepped back so that I would have room to enter.

"Come on in," he said while inspecting from head to toe.

I knew that he recognized me as well but just couldn't remember my name. As I neared him, I extended the pie and he accepted. I gently placed my hand on his shoulder and calmly spoke. "You and your family have my deepest condolences."

Sonny nodded his head in succession, sighed deeply then lowered his head. "Thank you and thanks for the pie."

I patted him on the shoulder once more as I turned away and slowly began my march through the living room. I stopped and greeted each of the family members and neighbors as I passed through. I was eagerly trying to get to where she was, Michelle. After reaching the kitchen I could hear the familiar voices of some of my neighborhood acquaintances. Suddenly, a voice from the dining room yelled, "They're in the basement and help yourself to something to eat."

I couldn't think about food at that moment, not with her being so near. It had been so long since I had seen her. I remember wondering what she now looked like. What if she had change drastically. What if she was a huge a whale or looking anorexic. *What if she looked nothing like I remembered*, I thought. My hands began to perspire as I approached the stairs. I stopped and stood at the top of the stairs momentarily before taking that first step. I walked down the stairs and entered the room of the awaiting eyes of most of the now young adults that I had grown up with. I swept the room not once but several times in disbelief. Out of all the smiling, greeting faces, Michelle's was not amongst them.

I kept my visit short after being informed that Fred had stopped by earlier and took Michelle out to help her clear her head. "*Yeah, clear his head*," I thought and I don't mean the one between his shoulders either. Well I guess somebody was doing some catching up. I chuckled to myself thinking, "*After all these years, I'm still jealous!*"

The funeral was held at Our Lady Queen of Peace Church. It was a lovely service. I arrived early enough for the viewing gowned in my Air Force "Dress Blues." It was the only suit that I had that I could fit after the military had buffed me up so much. I strolled up the center aisle and saw Fred sitting in the third row behind the family. He looked over at me with his usual cocky, arrogant smirk as to say, "Yep, I'm still screwing her." I smiled back at Fred but on this day my smile said, *"Maybe you are, but you won't be after I get in there."* His smirk dissipated as if he actually heard my thoughts.

After viewing Mrs. Taylor's body, I turned and advanced toward the family. I side stepped along the row giving my condolences and encouragement to everyone in my path. Finally, I was standing in front of Michelle. She looked up at me and through her blood shot, welled up eyes, she smiled.

"I'm so sorry for your loss Michelle, I really am," I said sincerely.

"Thank you so much Bobby, I know you are. You've always been so sweet."

"If you need anything, anything at all, don't hesitate to let me know, ok?"

"I will, I promise," she said then took my hand as she rose from her seat.

Michelle placed her arms around my waist and embraced me tightly. I held her close and placed my cheek against her soft hair. I know this sounds awful but I was beginning to achieve a slight erection. I remember thinking, *oh hell no, not now!* I slowly pulled away from her tight embrace although I didn't want to. She smiled at me and asked if I was coming by their home after the services. I told her that I would definitely be there. Now I know you're thinking, what a common, low down, disgusting, perverted bastard I must have been. The girls' mothers' body wasn't even cold yet and I was thinking of ways to use her death for my sexual advantage, what a bastard! So.

As I was saying... later that evening after changing out of my uniform I did return to the Taylor house. People were crowded inside eating, drinking, and talking. Once again, I was directed downstairs to the basement by one of her relatives. This time, the first face that I laid eyes on was Michelle's, the second one was Fred's.

I couldn't take my eyes off of Michelle the entire evening. She looked even better than I had imagined. Nope, she hadn't turned into the large, pretty-faced bear that I had imagined. Nor had she manifested into the Alien from the movie "Alien." On the contrary, her body had filled out and she was shapelier than ever. As I was locked on to her beauty, that bastard Fred was locked in on to me. Every statement or question that parted my lips was returned with a smug or snide comment from him. I had no other choice but to think that he must have gotten caught up in one of those time warps. He had to have had some type of flash back into junior high school. Well, I wasn't that little young kid that was impressed about how he played sports anymore. I had just come home from military training and in my back pocket was a fresh can of "Whoop Ass" that I wasn't afraid to pop open.

Michelle sensed the tension between the two of us and diplomatically tried to ration her time between us. She would look over at Fred and ask him about his mom and other relatives of his that she had met over the years. We chatted about my family and other neighbors that she hadn't seen since she had arrived back home. Fred and I continued to battle for position then suddenly Michelle said, "Sorry guys, this has been a long day, I hate to be rude but I am really tired. I really need to lie down for a while. How about I give you guys a call tomorrow?"

Fred nodded and I too gestured in agreement. As we headed up the stairs I inched up behind Michelle and whispered, "I've got one even better, how about I take you to the movies tomorrow, help you clear your mind a bit?"

Michelle looked back at me and smiled then nodded. I smiled and placed my hand on the small of her back as I assisted her up the stairs. As we inched up the stairs behind the others I once again whispered into her ear.

"Actually, I'll come by early tomorrow and take you for a ride. We can spend the day together. You know, make up for lost time. I'm sure you could use the break after all you've been through." She once again smiled and nodded.

After reaching the top of the stairs and making our way through the kitchen, I passed through the dining room and watched as Fred headed out the door. *"Now for that can of Whoop Ass,"* I thought. I gave Michelle a hug and rushed through the lingering crowd. I stepped out of the door and just like a thief in the night, Fred was gone. I stood there fuming, holding that can of "Whoop Ass" in one hand and the can opener in the other. Seems that he too realized that we were no longer kids.

That night I lay in my bed wondering if I would ever have the chance to have her as my own. Wondering what she ever saw in Fred and questioning why I just couldn't shake her from my every thought. It had been years and yet I still continue to think of her. Then I thought, *"There's only one thing left for me to do..."* I masturbated.

The next morning came as quickly as I did the night before. I rose and jumped in the shower. I stayed in longer than usual this morning. I got out and shaved my peach fuzz from under my chin and put on some of my father's cologne that was sitting on top of the sink. It was *"Old Spice."* I put on my clothes and stopped downstairs for a quick breakfast then picked up the phone and called Michelle.

"Hello," the voice answered.

It was her uncle Sonny.

"Hey Sonny, how are you feeling?" I politely asked.

"I'm hanging in there," he replied.

"Good... good. So, uh, is Michelle around?"

"Oh actually, she's not. Fred came by and took her down to the train station. She said that she just couldn't be here any longer. She said that being home and the funeral and all was just too much for her to handle right now so she was heading back to Atlanta. She called and checked the train schedule and found one that left this morning. She called Fred and he took her down to the station. She did tell me that if I saw you or if you called, to tell you that hopefully she'll see you when and if she comes back this way. She also wanted me to thank you for everything."

I stood there with my mouth hanging open in disbelief. I couldn't believe that she was gone, especially since I had the day planned out so perfectly. This would be the day that I told her exactly how I felt and this is how she left me, without a word and with that pompous prick, Fred? I was pissed! And once again Michelle was on my "*Most wanted to hate*" list. I'm sure that she probably told Fred what I was planning for her today and knowing him, he laughed his ass off inside. Once again, he was the victor. I was steaming. As I stood there ready to explode, I mentally removed that fresh can of "*Whoop Ass*" from my back pocket and scratched off the word "*Whoop.*" While gritting my teeth and gripping the can tightly, I etched the word *"Bust"* over top of where I had scratched out *"Whoop."* I was now holding a fresh can of *"Bust Ass"* and it had Fred's name on it. And I was holding it for the next time I saw Fred's face because I was definitely going to BUST HIS ASS! I didn't care if he was eighty-two years old when I saw him, he had an ass whuppin' comin'!

I remained home for several more days before returning to my next duty station. I reported to my technical training school. Here, we had a bit more freedom than in basic training. It was more like a job. We studied and performed hands on operations during the day. After our work day, we were free to do whatever we wanted in the evenings. This is where I took out most of the frustration that Michelle had left me with. It was easy pickings. The women on the base were in the same frame of mind that the men were. That was a rarity. They had been locked away for weeks just like us. They had long grueling days, just like us. And they were horny, just like us.

I first met Linda at the commissary. She was from Oxnard, California. I used to call her my little *"California Raisin"* because she was so dark. She too was a "291" or commonly known as "Commie." We were in the crypto/telecommunications field. It was pretty cool I guess. We were there to learn how to encrypt and decrypt transmitted messages. We did just that too, along with a few other things of course. We attended classes during the day and studied hard at night.

Linda was a really nice girl. She didn't swear or drink and would always try to encourage me to do the same. Linda had never had sex. That's right, Linda was still a virgin. So, I know you're asking yourself, "*If she was a virgin, what in the hell was I doing with her?*" Am I right? Well of course I tried to deflower her to answer your question but she was to have no part of that. Linda was saving herself for her husband and since I wasn't trying to become a husband, we became close friends. We would kiss amongst other things. And I did love that body of hers. There were other females on base that were giving it away like government cheese but there was something special about Linda.

Just about every evening, Linda and I would meet in the dining hall. We would sit and eat dinner while talking. After dinner we would discuss what we learned that day and what we were both planning for the future. At dusk, we would always walk down by the lake then return just after dark. We loved it down there. It was so peaceful and serene. It was a place where you could just forget about everything. You could just let go of yourself. We would sit down there for hours. We would talk, kiss, and fondle each other. Then just before we would head back to the barracks, Linda would always take me in her mouth and empty my insides. She was the best at oral satisfaction that I had ever had. Aww c'mon! Really? Did you really think that I wasn't getting some kind of sexual entertainment from her? In her mind, being a virgin meant that you had no vaginal penetration and she hadn't. Now as for that mouth... She could probably inhale all of New York State with one suck. She was very skilled in this area... the best. I would sometimes feel my rectum shift as she sucked me. I often thought that if not careful, she would just possibly suck a fart right through the head of my penis. I tell you, the girl was powerful. My testicles would sometimes stay up my stomach for three days after she was done with me. I don't know if they were stuck or just afraid to come back down, I just don't know. All I can tell you is that the girl seemed to be thirsty every evening. I bet she liked drinking from the water hose when she was a kid. *Ok, I was wrong for that.* I would usually walk back to the barracks with rubbery legs since Linda would almost drain the life out of me just prior to our departure from the lake. This went on during our entire stay there. This made for my best and most memorable portion of my Air Force career.

I had breezed through tech school, mostly dehydrated from extreme alcohol consumption and Linda's constant fluid draining. Still, I passed with honors and was now ready for assignment. I couldn't wait. I remember exploring all of the wonderful and exotic places in my mind. All the great adventures abroad. All of my mindful fantasies of exotic women and beautiful surroundings was quickly blown away after finally receiving my transfer orders. No, it was nowhere near where I was hoping for. It wasn't Japan, it wasn't Guam, hell, it wasn't even California. I was transferred to Andrews Air Force Base in Camp Springs, Maryland. What the hell!

My assignment at Andrews lasted for two years before leaving for not so sunny England. This too was not on my top list of places to be assigned but it was different and overseas. Most of the airmen there were stationed at Lakenheath Air Force base but our flight was assigned to the Royal Air Force Base Finningley. The base was small compared to most of the U.S. bases but it wasn't bad. Our barracks were like small townhomes which was pretty cool with one very nice benefit - the barracks were really close to the chow hall. It didn't take us long to get used to the base and surrounding area. We were a small group on the site but probably the rowdiest. The ladies of the Royal Air Base loved us Americans and that was exactly what I needed, something to keep my mind off of Michelle and home.

It wasn't long after arriving in merry old England that we airmen began frequenting the local pubs and night spots. This would occur nightly. It was pretty hard some mornings after the late nights of drinking and dancing but we managed. And becoming acquainted with the locals made it difficult to report for a twelve hour shift the following day. I would report for duty then rewind and playback the previous night's activities during my break. I met some pretty nice and unusual characters during my term there, especially the ladies. There were so many of these "British Birds" of a nice and entertaining character. Sweet, sexual women they were, but not sweet or nearly sexual enough to remove thoughts of Michelle from my mind.

I remained in England for two years before finally receiving the two things I wanted most during my military time, separation and discharge papers. I was more than ready too. Although life was good there, I was missing home. I did have my stable of reliable ladies and the work wasn't hard at all but still... it was time to go.

I packed up and headed for home. During my entire tour there I communicated with my parents but never attempted to return home. I guess the thought of that long grueling flight back to the states and the return was my deterrent.

Chapter 8 - Familiar Places

The city, neighborhood and the people were just the same as I had left it. The same guys hung out on the corner drinking beer and talking just as they had before I had left. The same dogs barked as I passed by the mutilated yards that they so diligently protected. Yes, everything was just how I remembered it. I pulled up about 4:30 that afternoon and climbed out of the sweltering interior of the Capital Cab that had me confined for the thirty-minute drive. Not only was it a pretty hot day out, the driver smelled of onions. I stood in front of the house that I had, for some reason, missed its company and gazed at its shabbiness for a brief moment before making my way toward the narrow staircase. I stood at the door, adjusted my uniform then wiped the sweat from my forehead just before stepping inside.

"Hey! Where's my girl? I know you're in here. You wouldn't have me fly all the way from England and not be home. So, where are you?" I yelled out cheerfully.

"Oh my goodness, Bobby, is that you?" her excited voice yelled from the top of the stairs.

"Yes ma'am, it's me. I'm back and back to stay! So, where's Pop?"

"You know him, he's out with Mr. Penny."

I placed my duffle bag down next to the couch and raced up the stairs taking them two at a time. I embraced my dear sweet mother as if I could never let her go. She held both sides of my face and kissed me gently on my cheek then smiled at me with teary eyes. She was happy, happy that her son was home.

"Oh Bobby, I'm just so happy to see you. You could have called, I would've at least cooked something for dinner that you liked. Look at you, all skin and bones," she went on while tapping her small hand on my chest.

"Ma, I'm fine. And the best thing is, I'm home, home for good."

Her face lit up. She pinched my cheeks then turned quickly and headed downstairs for the kitchen. No sooner as she had stepped into the kitchen then I could hear her rustling through the refrigerator trying to locate the items she needed in order to prepare a quick meal. Then suddenly a shriek trumpeted from the kitchen.

"I've got to call EVERYBODY!! I've got to let them know that you're home, my Bobby is home!"

Well, needless to say, nothing was cooked that evening. For over two hours she was on the phone with her sisters, cousins and a host of other relatives. My dad finally came in. He and Mr. Penny anxiously pulled me out onto the front porch. They wanted to hear about everything I had done overseas. I told them all the stories that I thought appropriate for the two gentlemen to hear and kept those rated "G." Suddenly the relatives started pouring in. Some came over within the hour of receiving the news toting food and spirits, while others just showed up and yes, it turned into a great welcome home party. We laughed, danced, ate and everyone welcomed me back home. I never felt more special than on that day.

Weeks had passed and I was just beginning to get settled in. My new focus was on a job, an apartment and someone to what I like to refer to as "spend time with." First on the agenda was an apartment because there was no way I was going to stay in the same house with my parents. After all those years of freedom, there was just no way I could live there. That was their sanctuary and that home came with strict rules. No females after nine o'clock, no females there if no one else was home and absolutely no PDA, personal displays of affection, in their presence. I'd go into a lifelong drought living there. I was a grown man now, with grown man needs and could make my own way. I just needed a layover until I got situated. The more my mother insisted I stay there with them, the harder I looked for a new job. Don't get me wrong, I loved them both with everything I have but you know what they say... "A man has needs!" That's right, every morning one of them would find me downstairs at the breakfast table eating a bowl of Cheerios and searching through the "Want Ads."

Several weeks had passed and still no luck with work. I had applied with every government agency in the Washington D.C. area. Every day, the same, nothing and I was at my wit's end. My mother was driving me crazy. She had even started knitting me a sweater with a matching knitted hat. *Don't give me that "ungrateful bastard" look! Would you wear them? I thought not.*

It was time, time to move before I got comfortable. I had some money saved and had given myself a month to find a job but tomorrow, job or not, I was finding a place.

I felt it before it happened. I got that warm, glowing feeling inside. Maybe I was just horny as hell, I'm not sure but the timing was definitely in sync with my feelings. The phone rang and I just knew it. I walked over to the wall mounted yellow contraption and pick up the handset and answered.

"Hello."

"Yes, may I speak with Mr. Robert Mason please?"

"Yes, yes this is he, this is Robert Mason."

"Hi Mr. Mason, this is Mrs. Samuels from Navy Personnel. You interviewed for a position here as a Communications Specialist and we would like to schedule an interview with you."

"Sure, that would be great!"

"Great, how does Monday sound? Would you available on Monday?"

"Yes, Monday is fine."

"Ok, then we will be expecting to see you then."

This was the best news that I could have ever received. Well, that and Michelle's return. I wanted to tell my mother the good news but I knew that she would only worry her head off then push her worry over on me. She would want to make sure that I was ready for the interview and want to know what I was going to wear, how I was getting there and anything else associated with that meeting. I decided to keep the interview to myself.

Monday morning arrived like a flash. I caught a cab over to the Washington Navy Yard. The building was pretty old and shabby but pretty standard as military buildings go. I entered through the two glass double doors into a drab foyer then walked up to the receptionist and stated my business there. I signed the log sheet and was issued a temporary visitor's badge before waiting for my escort. After waiting several minutes, a young man entered the room and quickly rushed over to where I stood. He extended his hand to me while producing a bright smile.

"Mr. Mason?"

"Yes," I replied while shaking his hand.

"Right this way. We didn't expect you this early but we're ready for you," he said while extending his arm toward the direction of the doors.

After entering through the doors that lead to the office area, the young man escorted me to the large conference room at the end of the corridor. He opened the conference room door and I stepped inside to the awaiting group of interviewers. It was a team of four, three men and one woman. I was greeted by the gentleman that sat at the head of the table then each member introduced themselves. I introduced myself, then sat at the table and the interrogation began. I was questioned on my skills and abilities for over thirty minutes. There was one interviewer that seemed to have a tenseness about her. That's right, I said "her." The young woman would ask me questions but would seem to be a bit annoyed each time that I answered her question correctly. She would always follow up my answer with a "Why would you take that approach" or "Did you observe this in the work place or do you actually have hands on experience doing this?" *What in the hell kind of questions are these?* I remember asking myself but never the less, I rolled through them like nothing at all. After all, I knew the material. It was what I did. I had the knowledge and the experience. And even thought "Ms. Tight Ass" was trying to trip me up with her strange line of questioning, I prevailed. The other interviewers seemed to be pleased with my answers and I was confident that I had answered their questions thoroughly and correctly.

At the end of the interview, I was asked if I had any questions for them and of course I did. I know what you're thinking and strangely enough, you're right. I wanted so badly ask who was in charge of pulling the stick out of the young lady with the attitude's ass but instead I settled on a few standard questions about travel and health care, that sort of thing. But you thought right. I see you're beginning to understand me more as you continue reading.

The interview had gone well. After it was over, I remember feeling confident on how I had nailed it and how I was a shoe in for the job.

Several days had passed and I began to accept reality. *Guess I hadn't nailed it after all*, I thought. I had applications submitted at several military installations but I really wanted that one. It would have been perfect. The commute would have been easy from wherever I lived and the starting pay was great. I don't know but I had a feeling that it had everything to do with "Ms. Tight Ass." It was time to get back to the drawing board. I couldn't wait any longer. I pulled out my resume and decided to try to beef it up a bit and perhaps re-apply at some of the places where I really wanted to work or maybe try an employment agency. I was at my wit's end.

I was now three days into the next week which felt like two years at home. And Dad was beginning to give me that look. You know, the "You've been here long enough to have a job but your unemployed ass is still living in my house and eatin' my food so it's time for your freeloading ass to pay some rent" look. Something had to give and soon.

That Thursday was like Christmas. I was contacted by phone that morning. I'm not sure what took them so long but it was just as I had thought, I had nailed the interview. The young woman called and offered me the job which without hesitation, I accepted. As I stood there listening to the woman provide me with reporting instructions and other pertinent information about salary and vacation. Then she stated those words that I had been waiting to hear: "Mr. Mason, if you have any questions, please feel free to contact me. We will be looking forward to seeing you on Monday the 22nd."

I hung up the phone and it happened. A smile appeared on my face that I couldn't remove then I thought... "*Apartment.*"

The following morning the quest was on. I got dressed, had breakfast, grabbed Mom's car keys and headed out in search of my new residence. I remembered a cluster of apartment buildings just off Pennsylvania Avenue just across the Maryland state line. I wanted to be just far away from my mom and dad to do my dirt without any surprise visits. They weren't about to drive that far without phoning to ensure I would be home.

I arrived at the Sussex Square Apartments that afternoon and had decided that this would be my new home. I had visited three other apartment complexes but none had the look and feel of comfort of this one. It was a little more expensive but well worth it. I filled out the paperwork with the property manager and left the application fee along with a check for the deposit. Two days later, I was informed that the apartment was mine. I immediately drove out and signed the remaining paperwork and collected the keys to my new apartment. For some strange reason the property manager wanted me to provide her with a move-in date. I found that to be odd at first but later found out that it was for security reasons. Seems that someone in the past had backed up a "U-Haul" truck to one of the buildings and cleaned out a resident's belongings and everyone thought that they were there to move the person out. Although I had no furniture, I was more than eager to move in so I just blurted out, "Two weeks from Saturday." The property manager jotted the date down in her log. She placed the folder with copies of my paperwork down on the desk in front of me along with the keys to the apartment. She stood, smiled then shook my hand.

"Enjoy your new apartment, Sir. And please, feel free to let us know if you have any problems," she said sincerely.

I shook her hand, smiled and nodded in agreement then snatched up the keys and the folder and made my exit. This was it!

A long slow week had passed. Not scheduled to move in to my new place for another week, I was bored. As I sat quietly on the couch awaiting my mother's return from choir rehearsal. I could hear his loud and raspy voice shouting to someone walking down the street.

"If you're not a Redskins fan, you're with a losing team!" he yelled.

It was none other than Donald, my childhood sex instructor. I crawled off of the sofa and walked over to the back door. I peered across the alley but saw no one.

"You wanna stop makin' all that noise over there man," I yelled.

Without the presence of his image I could hear him clearly shout, "Who is that? Is that you Bobby?"

"None other."

"Man, get your butt over here. I didn't know you were back."

The dark silhouette stepped outside the door and rushed down the stairs. I then stepped outside, trotted down the stairs and out the gate into the alley to meet him. As he approached me, he flicked his cigarette in my direction then walked up me and gave me a big bear hug. He was like a brother to me.

"Are you back for good?" he asked.

"Yep, done. Uncle Sam has gotten all he's gonna get from me as a military man."

"Wow, that's great man. I missed you bro."

"Yeah, I missed you too man."

"Damn if you did. No letters, no postcards or phone calls... you didn't miss me."

"No man really, I did. I thought about you often. Especially every time I hooked up with a lady and stuck it in the right place. I would always think to myself... *thank you Donald, thank you*."

"Yuck man, that's both nasty and weird. Don't think about me when you're pokin' some chick man, that's just sick!"

We stood there laughing and talking for over an hour before he said the words that lit my soul on fire.

"You know your girl's in town, staying at her mom's," he said smiling.

"Who, Michelle?"

"Yep, the one and only," the raspy voice replied.

"Man, I haven't seen her in a while. How's she doin', have you seen her?"

"Of course. Same Michelle as always. She still looks the same and still sweet as ever. Hey, you owe that some get back don't you? Don't you want to show her that you finally figured out where to put it now?" he said while laughing hysterically.

"Man, that girl never walked the same after I was done with her, I used to tear that up!"

"Yeah, guess it was hard to walk with a hole in her thigh the size of a pencil point," he said while chuckling.

"Yeah, and I changed her navel from an 'outty' to an 'inny' in just five short strokes," I said while laughing.

"Real short strokes..."

"Man, if she had only laid still long enough, I would've figured it out," I said still laughing.

"Yeah, and if my aunt had balls... she'd be my uncle!" Donald belted out.

We both began to laugh uncontrollably. It was like we had never been apart. Donald was exactly the same Donald that I had left. I wondered if Michelle was. Donald and I talked for a little while longer before I mustered up enough courage to go see Michelle. I told him that I'd stop by later and we could catch up some more and he agreed.

I headed back into the house and locked the back door. Mom still hadn't returned from choir rehearsal and dad was upstairs still snoring. I went upstairs and cleaned myself up then changed my clothes. I wanted to look my best for her. I slipped on my favorite jeans, a shirt and my mustard colored earth shoes. I sprayed a little English Leather cologne on then rushed down the stairs and out the front door. As I bent the corner in the direction of Michelle's house I could hear the familiar voice in the distance. "Hey stranger!" I knew that voice all too well. It was Robyn. I couldn't believe my ears. After she had left for college, I didn't think that I would ever see, let alone feel her again. Now my "love/lust" meter had kicked in. Do I wave and continue up to see Michelle or do I pause and line up what should be a sure thing? Let's face it, I was hittin' that right! *"Bobby, just wave and catch up with her later,"* I thought to myself. I didn't know how long Michelle would be here. My decision was made.

I turned and waved to Robyn, "What's going on lady? It's been a long time."

Robyn continued in my direction. It was already too late for me to just walk off. I crossed over to the other side of the street to meet her.

"How have you been?" I asked as I gave her a huge hug.

"I've been great! Your mother didn't tell you that I came by several times to see when you were coming home?"

"Yeah, she did but I didn't think you were still here. Thought you had already returned to school. How was it, school that is?"

"I missed you the entire time."

"Well, we've got a lot of catching up to do."

"We've got more than that to do," she mumbled while rubbing my arm.

"Oh yeah, I've missed that more than you know. I just got my own place and you know I can't wait to show it to you," I said while smiling and dangling my ring of keys in front of her face.

"Really? Well let's see how we can break it in," she said grinning.

"Did you study mind reading or become psychic while you were up at that school because you surely just read my mind," I said while grinning.

"They say great minds think alike. So where are you off to?"

Ok, I had just got my regular thruster back on lock and I know that I was sure to ruin it if I told her that I was off to see Michelle. So, since she said I had such a great mind, I did what any great mind would do... I lied.

"Oh nowhere, was gonna stop by Donald's and see what's going on with him but if you're not doing anything later, let's hang out."

"I'd like that," she said while smiling that sneaky smile of hers.

"Actually, I'm waiting for my mom to get back then I'm heading over to the furniture store to see what I can find. A lady's touch might help. We can even stop by the apartment and you can check it out first so you can get an idea of what I need."

"So, is that code for 'Carpet burns?'" she asked, again with that sneaky smile.

"Again, can't get anything by you. They really taught you well up there," I said while glaring at her breast.

We hugged again and said our goodbyes both knowing that we would be tearing into each other's flesh within the hour. Oh, what a feeling.

I turned and started back up the hill toward Michelle's. Her Uncle Sonny lived there now but it was still owned by Michelle. I looked back as I neared Donald's to see if Robyn was still in view. She wasn't. I continued past Donald's and crossed the street to my ex-thigh burning shop. I walked up and stopped in front of the door to make any last minute adjustments to my hair and apparel. I felt pretty good. I took a deep breath, cleared my throat then knocked on the door. A short moment later, I could hear someone walking toward the door. The deadbolt turned and the door was opened. There standing before me was the woman that still took my breath away. She was stunning. Just feeling that way about her made me feel like a sap. That's right, a real "head-over-heels" chump. This woman couldn't give a fat rat's ass about me and here I am feeling like a little puppy that just got rewarded for pissing on the paper, damn! I mean really? I felt like I couldn't find my ass with both of my hands any time she was near me.

Michelle opened the door wider and smiled. "Well I'll be. I've been asking about you. Nobody seemed to know where you were or how you were doing. Come on in. How are you?"

I was smiling from ear to ear and even getting a little stimulated. I know, right? Maybe she did give a fat rat's ass about me after all.

"I'm good. I just got out of the Air Force. I was overseas for a while but other than that, I haven't been up to much."

"Yeah, I remember somebody telling me that you were in the military and you were somewhere overseas. Where were you?"

"I was over in England for a couple of years, just got back home a few weeks ago and I gotta say, it's good to be back home."

"England, huh? How did you like it over there? I bet those Brit chicks were all over you, huh? A good looking young man like yourself, I know they couldn't resist."

"Nah, not me but it was alright over there. It's nothing like being home though."

"Have you seen any of the old gang since you've been home?"

"I just saw Donald, he told me you were here."

"Well I'm glad you stopped by. Look at you all grown up and looking good too."

"Thanks, but you always look good. How long are you in town?"

"Just a couple more weeks. We should get together before I head back."

Now you know with that being said, my "Dickometer" switched into "auto."

"Yes, we should," I said as calmly as I could.

"What are doing this evening, I'm free?" she asked.

"Well, as soon as my mother gets back home with the car I've got to head out to look for some furniture for my apartment."

"You need some help picking out some furniture? I've got good taste when it comes to that and besides I could stand to get out of this house for a while."

Damn it! She's about to blow my good sure thing here, Robyn, I shouted in my mind. Michelle was a "I don't know" but was my preference. I still remembered how she just up and left the last time she was here and without a word. She was a maybe at best where Robyn and I would be peeling the paint off the walls five minutes after entry into the empty apartment. And if Robyn found out that I dropped her to take Michelle in her place, that sure thing would've become nothing but a sweet memory. I couldn't chance it. I looked at Michelle and mustered up every ounce of strength that I had and said, "I'll come and pick you up when my mom gets home." I know, I know... I'm just a sucker for this woman.

Michelle smiled and said she would be ready. We embraced and I made my exit. As I walked back down the hill toward home I tried to figure out what I was going to tell Robyn. She so looked forward to going with me to pick out furniture and to leave the apartment with a mound of carpet lint in her hair and a tender carpet burn at the small of her back. What was I doing?

Later that evening my mother returned from rehearsal. I gathered my things and headed downstairs to greet her.

"Where are you off to in such a rush young man, hot date?" she asked looking over the top of her eyeglasses.

"No, just going to hang out for a little while with some old friends," I responded.

You see, I couldn't tell her that I was going to pick out new furniture because she would have given me such a lecture about my aunt Debbie's furniture downstairs in the basement that I could use temporally until I saved up more money. Hell no. This was going to be my bachelor pad until Michelle came back for good.

Mother smiled and passed me her car keys. I gave her a peck on the cheek and smiled back.

"I won't be too late," I said then rushed out of the door.

I hopped in the car and started the engine, kicked it into "drive" and pulled around the corner to collect my precious. I double parked the car and trotted up to the front door. The door opened as I neared. It was Uncle Sonny.

"Michelle, the guy from around the corner is back," he grumbled. *"Now why is it that he could remember Fred's name but not mine and he's known me longer?"* I thought while looking at his snarled-up face oddly. Michelle stepped through the doorway and greeted me once again with a huge hug.

"You ready?" I asked eagerly.

She nodded in affirmation and off we went. I opened the passenger side door and waited until she was safely inside. I rushed around to the driver's side and opened the door and pounced on the seat. Before starting the car, I inspected the area for Robyn. Once realizing the coast was clear, I threw the car in gear and sped off.

Chapter 9 - The Re-acquaintance

Michelle appeared to be just as excited as I was but for different reasons I'm sure. As the car rolled along she talked about sofas and curtain patterns. All I could think about was getting her out of her clothes and how much ointment I was going to need for the carpet burns on my knees the following morning. Michelle kept on about placemats for the table and lamps until suddenly she said something very unexpected. "Let's go by your place first."

My eyes lit up! Here I am thinking that I would probably have to coax her after furniture shopping and dinner to stop by there. No, she wanted to get right to it. Maybe she had thought about me as I did her. Maybe she wanted to right the same wrong that I did from all those years ago. Hell, maybe she was just horny. It didn't matter what the case was, I was willing and ready!

I made a quick "U" turn on Marlboro Pike and a fast left onto Brookes Drive which led to Pennsylvania Avenue. I was now moving through the traffic like Mario Andretti. I was now getting closer to what I had waited so long for.

My heart was racing faster than ever as we pulled into the parking lot. I was already beginning to feel a little heat downstairs just from the anticipation. I jumped out of the car and rushed around to her to open the door but she had beat me to it. *"Oh yeah, she's ready!"* I thought. She climbed out of the car and took hold of my arm and I led her inside the building and upstairs to my castle. I fumbled with the keys trying to unlock the door as my hands were now perspiring like a one legged man in an ass kicking contest. I was so ready for this. I opened the door and pushed it as wide as it would open to allow the light from the hallway in as I had not yet acquired a lamp in the living area.

Michelle stepped in, looked around for only a moment then walked over to the large window of the living room. I closed the door and walked into the dining room and flicked the light switch. The dim illumination from the bulb was somewhat irritating but sufficient enough for the tour. Michelle walked into the kitchen and turned the light on for only a brief moment then stepped over into the bathroom. Only poking her head in the bedroom for a second or two seemed to have been enough time to make her assessment of the area. I walked back into the living room and waited. Making one more stop into the bathroom for her last study then into the dining area. She stood there looking around then turned to me and smiled.

"A nice wooden dinette set would look nice under this light and a couple of pictures on the walls in here would give it some character, don't you think?" she asked while moving about, gesturing with her hands.

I stood there quietly thinking, *"Damn, she just wanted to survey the place for design ideas? I knew I should've brought Robyn. I would have been knee deep in flesh right now."*

Now realizing that the "Bangathon" that I was so desperately hoping for was probably not going to happen, I shut down. My mind went elsewhere. I was now thinking more than ever what a mistake I had made. I mean, Michelle is the love of my life but what I needed that night wasn't love... I needed to sweat, scream and smile.

"Bobby?!" she shouted.

"Oh sorry, I was just trying to visualize the table and pictures. Uh yeah, I think that would look nice," I responded trying to look interested.

Michelle went on about what would look nice in the bathroom and the bedroom. I never moved from my spot. I just stood there listening to her rant on about furniture, pictures and lamps. Hell, at that point I was ready to go to the damn furniture store.

Finally, Michelle was done with her observation and assessment of apartment requirements. She turned off the dining room light and walked over to me. I dug in my pocket to retrieve the car keys and turned toward the door.

"I love the way the moonlight shines into this window, I'd never turn on any lights in here. I'd probably sit out here in the dark most of the time. It's so soothing," she said in a soft sweet voice.

"Yeah, I guess it is," I replied then started for the door.

Michelle reached over and took my hand. I turned around and the way she peered into my eyes stopped my heart. I couldn't help but to think, *this was it*! I stepped closer to Michelle and placed my hand on her shoulder. I gazed deep into her eyes and spoke as gentle as I could, "You know I've never stopped thinking about you. I know we were just kids but there really hasn't ever been anybody who has touched me the way you have. I believe I've been waiting for you ever since."

I wanted to tell her that I loved her but thought it might have been a little too much so I decided to take a different angle. Michelle began to speak but I interrupted her.

"You were my first love Michelle, my true love. People say that you can't help who you love."

I felt that at that moment, it was the perfect time to move in. I moved my face closer to hers and closed my eyes. As I zeroed in on her lips. I pulled her closer.

"Uh, Bobby..." she whispered.

I opened my eyes with my lips still puckered.

"Yes," I answered.

"Uh... that's about the nicest thing anybody has EVER said to me. I'm truly touched. You too were my first love but..."

"I know you live far away but I believe we can still make it work. We can at least give it a try," I said trying not to sound too desperate.

"No, but..."

"But what? I see no reason why couldn't just give it a try. I could come spend time with you, you could come here a spend time with me. I could even look into finding a job in Atlanta if you don't want to come back here," I said.

"No, but..."

"But what Michelle, why can't we at least try?"

Michelle looked down at the floor then slowly back into my eyes. The words she uttered to me on that day, I'll never forget. I looked into her eyes then for some reason at her pretty full lips. I still wanted to kiss her badly. I watched as her lips moved and the words poured out. It was as if they spilled from her mouth in slow motion with a loud echo spiraling down deep into my heart.

"My husband," she whispered faintly.

I stood there speechless. Frozen and in shock. I couldn't move or speak for at least five minutes. As I returned to reality I thought, *"Damn, I just poured my heart out to this woman, what a jackass!"* I wanted to crawl up under a rock and have somebody, anybody, drive a tank or bulldozer over it. I could no longer look her in the eyes. I felt like such an idiot.

After collecting myself, I turned to her. Now looking down at the floor, I spoke.

"I don't understand Michelle. If you're married and happy, why are you here with me now?"

"You asked me to come with you to pick out furniture remember?"

"Yeah, but..."

"Bobby, I really do like you too but I was only being a friend. I love decorating and I really thought that you could use my help. I didn't realize that this was being transmitted as a mix signal, I'm so sorry if I gave you the wrong impression. If things were different I would be more than interested but I love my husband," she said in an apologetic voice.

"No Michelle, I'm sorry. I didn't know and you never said anything that misleading, I just thought..."

"I thought you knew that I was married. I forgot, you've been gone for a long time too. Everyone knows. Let's put this behind us and just forget that this ever happened, alright?"

I kept my eyes focus on the carpet then back up to Michelle's huge brown eyes then muttered, "Alright."

"Now how about we go pick you out some nice furniture for this place?" she asked in a cheerier voice.

"No, I don't feel much like furniture shopping right now. How about I take you home and maybe do it another day if that's ok with you?"

Michelle could see clearly that I was heartbroken. She nodded in agreement and we walked out of the apartment. We climbed back into the car and I drove her home. We were both silent the entire ride.

I pulled in front of her house and did not get out of the car. She leaned over and kissed me on the cheek.

"Again, I'm so sorry Bobby, I really am."

I could tell that she was being sincere and could feel my pain herself. She got out of the car and I watched her as she made her way up the walkway to the front door. After she had made it safely inside I slowly pulled off.

Now only thinking of doing nothing but going into a dark room and drinking until I passed out. I pulled up in front of the house and cut the car off. I sat there thinking about what had just happened and how I made such a fool of myself. With all that had just occurred, I knew that even still, I loved her.

After several more minutes of thinking I finally pulled myself together and out of the car. I walked through the gate and up to the door. I knocked softly. She opened the door and smiled. "You ready?" I asked.

"Yeah, give me a sec," she replied.

I stood on the porch as I could hear her yelling up to her mom. "I'll be back in a little while, I'm running up to Marlo's with Bobby," she shouted.

I could faintly hear her mother acknowledging her. *Now surely you didn't think I was going home? Besides, I didn't drink and the only dark room I was going to lay in was the one in my new apartment. I still had a few carpet burns to inflict.*

Yep, Robyn and I left and headed straight for the apartment. And I'm sure you know we never made it to the furniture store. And the only assessments that Robyn made in that apartment that night, was how the moonlight shined on her toenails as she pointed them toward the ceiling. I came to realize one thing in particular that night... furniture shopping was fun.

The following day was very different from the day before, I was not angry nor disappointed with Michelle, instead I had feelings of respect and admiration for her. She honored her husband enough not to succumb to my advances. I wanted her even more than before now. That's exactly how strong of a woman I would want as a wife. Of course, I realized that she would never be that woman.

Michelle remained at Sonny's for eight more days. During that time, I was forgiven and we enjoyed each other's company. Nothing else was said about that night. We went to the movies, out to dinner and even to the miniature golf course. It was good times but as always, all good things must come to an end. Michelle was leaving in the morning.

After her departure things had pretty much gone back to normal. I finally purchased furniture for my place that Robyn so nicely picked out and even bought a new car, a Toyota Celica. I had started my new job and yes, still penetrating Robyn's hot steaming body every chance that I got. It wasn't a bad life, not at all. Actually, it was quite perfect, except for one thing, Michelle. How or why, still remained a mystery for me but she still had my heart. She had my nose wide open and from what, a few months of heated kissing, panting and thigh humping? No way, I'm a grown man now and I'm still thinking about my childhood sweetheart as if she were the best lay in the world, that's just pathetic. *That must've been a really soft thigh and moist too, damn.*

Chapter 10 - Scared Straight

As with all things, time had passed but most things remained the same with some ever so slight changes in my life. I had now been working at the Navy Yard for thirteen years. Robyn had finally gotten tired of me because she was looking for a real commitment over the years and I just wasn't into her for anything much more than a straight "stop and pop." She was now married with four children living at her parents' house with her second husband. I had been living at the same apartment but it was now time for a change. I decided on setting my goals a little higher. Yep, I decided to stay in the area and purchase a home. I was still set on living and being alone without any real commitment. There were plenty of women to hang out with and who were happy with just interacting in the physical only but I had had my fill. After Carol, I was done!

Oh, I didn't tell you about Carol, did I? You're just gonna love this chick. You might wanna go and freshen up that cup of coffee, tea or top off that glass of wine you're sippin' on before I tell you about this one. I'll wait...

Alright, you're all set? Ok check this out... I first met Carol at the Home Depot. It was about two years prior to my move. I had decided to paint my place so I headed over to the Home Depot to purchase the paint and supplies that I needed. As I walked up to the counter, standing before me is the sexiest, sweetest looking mocha chocolate woman that I had ever seen. She walked up to me and in her sweet, sexy, Jamaican accent she says, "Yes Sir, and how may I help you today?"

I stood there frozen for a second before answering.

"Yes, I need some paint and a few supplies to paint an entire apartment," I replied.

She proceeded to step from behind the counter and my eyes instantly began to water. The onion below her back was perfectly shaped and rocked from side to side so sexy with each stride. with my eyes watering, I followed that sexy onion over to the color chart on the side wall. Two months later she was trying to move in.

Little by little with each visit Carol would bring and leave a piece of clothing. It wasn't long before she was asking for a drawer. Next it was space in my closet to hang a couple of dresses in case we were going out somewhere nice so she wouldn't have to go back home to change. This went on for several months and I really didn't mind it much after all, she was so sexy and passionate that she was more than enough for my sexual desires to feast on. Plus, she did that thing with her tongue... *Never figured out exactly what it was that she did or how she did it. All I know is... she could send me to Uranus with it.*

She now had enough stuff that could fit into a manageable size box. You know, for easy transport. So, I allowed her to feel pretty much at home. That is, until the crazy beast inside her started rearing its ugly head.

Carol was pretty calm in the beginning of our relationship but the closer we got, the more insecure she got. The jealousy became uncontrollable and at times, she would just go into a rage. I was warned on many occasions that she would "cook my head" if she ever caught me with another woman. Now, I didn't know what that meant, all I know is that I didn't want any part of that. I didn't know if it was meant for the big head or the little head. One thing was for certain, she wasn't bluffing. When I inquired as to the meaning of the statement, she looked up at me as if I had choked the life out of her first born and spoke calmly, "Don't you worry dear, you'll know when I come for you."

Now what in the hell does that mean? No, tell me because I sure as hell don't know.

I dealt with that woman for over eight months before having to call the police to have her deranged ass escorted out of my place and file a restraining order. I would've done it much sooner but the psycho could make a mean curry goat stew and her rice and peas were to die for. Well, and as I said earlier, not only could she do the thing with her tongue but she could also do this thing with her... well you know what I mean. I believe that was my first experience with a "Snapper." And any man that's ever had one will tell you, you just can't seem to ever walk away from a "Snapper." I mean honestly, a woman could have gone out and killed three people, with one of the three being a man's own mama. Addicted to that snapper, he'd be sitting there debating if he should turn her in. He'd be thinking to himself, "*I mean, what's done is done. I can't go back and change the past. It's too late now, Mama's gone but... the snapper... the snapper is still here and alive!*" That woman could literally get away with murder and why? Because of the muscle control that she possesses between her legs. *I never introduced her to my mother.*

I remember the first sexual encounter between Carol and me. I remember sliding her panties down and boom! The pubic hair popped from their restraint like a mushroom cloud. It kind of reminded me of the old "Jiffy Pop" popcorn poppers. They would explode open once the popcorn was ready, well so did her pubes. There was so much hair! I looked down and didn't know if it was her flower or the top of Don Kings head. It was all over the place.

Just as I was thinking of declining the prize, Carol reached up and took me in her hand. And what the hell she did, to this day I can't even do to myself and believe me, I've tried. That woman almost brought me to an orgasm with her hand! Suddenly she stopped and gripped the sides of my hips with both hands and pulled me toward the Don King hair. I tried to fight back... *Ok, are you really believing that part, really?   You know damn well I dove right into that hot flesh. There was no fighting back, not from my nasty ass. I did it, so there.*

I slid myself deep into the Don's hair. That's when I felt it. The Don took hold of me and with every stroke that I gave it, it stroked back. It was effortless for her. It was if she had another hand inside her. I was maintaining myself while inside her even as she snapped that thing on me. Then she decided to really give it to me. Carol began to move her hips slow but powerful and Don began to snap harder and grip tighter with each grind. She stopped suddenly and moaned out, "Ya mon," then the Don took hold of me and began to pulsate. I tried to pull back for another stroke but it wouldn't let me. That's right, it wouldn't let me. The Don was gripped around me like a vice. Then, Carol's eyes rolled to the back of her head as the wetness began to cover me then I was slowly released.

Carol lay there with the look of pure satisfaction on her face. This look only lasted for a brief moment before Carol was back to moving those hips and letting the Don do its thing once again. It gripped, stroked and massaged me until I could take no more. Carol knew exactly what she was doing. I tried to hold on but couldn't. Yep you guessed it... I blew like a rocket. I gotta tell you, the girl was a sex master.

I became obsessed with the Don after that. I craved the Don daily. I needed the Don. Carol just happened to be the keeper of the Don... and her ass was crazy.

After Carol was removed from my apartment all kinds of strange occurrences followed. I would come home from work and find dead birds on my windowsill and the week after she left, I couldn't taste anything for over a week. And to this day, I still believe that it was her who wiped the chicken blood over the hood of my car and the door to my apartment. I needed rehab to wean myself off of the Don. Even today I'm still taking it one day at a time. I still look for her in the shadows ready to pounce out and "cook my head." And I guess it's needless to say, but I became a Lowe's man after that! And to this day, my eye twitches every time I drive by a Home Depot or think of that woman. Hell, it's twitching right now.

After Carol, I didn't date for a long while. Sure, I had my go to, but not a relationship. After all, she already had three kids and an ex-husband. I wanted no parts of that. Any lady that I met, including her, I would tell them that I was married and my wife was stationed overseas. Of course, her name was Michelle. This kept everything in perspective.

Chapter 11 - Shoot the Stork

Two long years had passed and I was still a bit hesitant about dating. My "go to" who only lived a couple of buildings down from me was even beginning to want more. My ghost military wife who had never visited was not helping my situation with her either. I knew it was finally time to cut the tie but after all this time, she knew my body like a book. She knew exactly what made me tick and which button to push to make me blow! This was truly one of the hardest decisions of my life to make. I remember sitting in the living room contemplating what to do when the knock came to the door. I got up from the couch, walked over to the door and looked through the peep hole. It was as if she was reading my mind. It was as if she had known that I was thinking about her. I glared out for a brief second. There she stood with her arms folded looking in both directions as if she had just committed a crime. It was my "go to", Karen. Seems as if fate had made my mind up for me. I opened the door and she quickly stepped in. I looked at her strangely as she looked down at the floor. Maybe she had decided to end it as well. I guess that would save me the trouble and she could be the "bad guy" instead. I had just decided that if that was what she wanted to say then I would slip on my most heartbroken facial mask just before saying... "I understand." I did want her to make me tick just once more though before it was over but I guessed that would be out of the question.

"Hey! What's wrong, are you alright?" I said reaching over raising her chin upward.

"Not really," she replied lowering her eyes back toward the floor.

"Come on, talk to me, what's the matter?"

"I didn't mean for this to happen, really I didn't."

"Are the kids alright?"

"Yeah, they're fine."

"Then what? I've never seen you like this."

"I'm so sorry Bobby."

"Ok, here it comes. Let me get my look ready," I thought.

"Sorry about what baby?" I asked while phasing into my "crushed" look.

She looked up slowly. But instead of dumping me, she slapped me with the hardest blow that a woman could hit a man with.

"Yes, I am so sorry. I know we talked about this and I told you I'd be careful but I guess I wasn't."

"Careful with what? No... Surely you're not saying..."

"I'm late! I'm sorry. I was being as careful as I could. I don't know what went wrong!" she said now crying uncontrollably.

"How can you be late, we always wore protection?"

"No, remember that time when my mother was on her way from her house bringing the kids back and you stopped over and kept wanting a quickie?"

"I did?"

"Yes, you did. I said 'no' and you said, 'Aww c'mon baby let me just put the tip in then.' You went on and on about how you would be quick so I finally gave in. You bent me over the couch and slid more than just the tip in."

"But I pulled out."

"I guess you didn't pull out quick enough. Maybe if you had only put the tip in, you would have been quick enough."

I was now the one staring at the waves of fabric in the carpet. "How in hell did this happen?" I mumbled but I guess we all know how it happened. And she was right, I remembered that night as if it were yesterday. I remembered clearly because during that exchange, I sprang my wrist from gripping too tightly on the back of the couch during my orgasm.

Without any hesitation at all my mind had begun evaluating my future. It displayed a glimpse of me walking through an already crowded grocery store with kids on every side of the shopping cart that I was pushing. Other visions similar to this streamed through my mind as I stood there speechless. I tried to speak but couldn't. I should have known better than to even sneeze next to the "baby making machine." It was obvious that Karen was fertile as Kentucky soil, daaaamn!

After gathering myself, I looked up at Karen and mustered everything within me to utter these words, "Everything's gonna be ok."

"No, no it won't," she whined.

"Don't worry, we'll figure something out."

"Like what?"

"I don't know, we just need to take some time to think here," I said then lowered my head once more.

"I'm so sorry. I didn't mean to bring this on you. What will you tell your wife?"

"My wife, what wife? what in the hell is she talking about, wife?" I thought. I had totally forgot that I had told her that. I responded with the most sophisticated answer that I could think of at that moment, "I don't know."

"I've already got three kids and I know this sounds horrible but I'm not sure that I could handle another one," she continued whining.

"Look, just go home for now and think on it, and I'll do the same. We'll talk later alright?"

Karen nodded then headed for the door. I opened the door and placed my hand on the small of her back. Just as she was exiting, she turned and threw her arms around me. She was squeezing me so tight I could hardly breathe.

"You're not angry with me, are you? I didn't mean for this to happen please believe that," she said still squeezing me tightly.

"I know and no, I'm not angry."

I had lied, I was mad as hell! Karen turned and walked out and I stood in the doorway and watched her until she was out of sight.

All of the thoughts that seemed to somehow vanish quickly returned. I was now seeing myself sitting in my car with it stuffed with kids and Karen then up walked Michelle. My heart sank. That did it for me. At that very moment I did something that I hadn't done in years. I fell to my knees and prayed! I prayed to God asking him to please not let that woman be pregnant, not with my child anyway. *Oh don't judge. Don't even act like you've never fell to your knees when you thought you've just been hit with the hardest punch that life has to offer. Funny, we all wait 'til then. I begged, pleaded and just like you... I promised I'd never do it again.*

Two days had passed and I hadn't spoken to Karen. I tried to call but just couldn't. I hadn't even spoken to my mother since the news, I couldn't find the courage to tell her. I guess I felt that she would be so disappointed in me. Karen knew what kind of guy I was, she knew that I'd take care of the baby. I think she was more concerned with another baby to care for in a house with no husband or man to call her own. Although she was my "go to", I knew she had developed feelings for me but would never let them show in fear of me terminating our non-existent relationship. Now it seems that I would be stuck in some type of relationship with her after all.

I finally mustered up enough courage to go visit my parents, not to break the news but just to visit. I needed to see them. I wasn't sure how I was going to act or what I was going to say to them. But I knew that I'd better have it together when I got there because my mother would surely detect that there was something going on with me. She could always seem to know when there was something wrong. I don't know, maybe it was just women's intuition. All I know is, she could sniff out a problem better than a bloodhound sniffing out a rabbit.

I still had some thinking to do and I was still banking on that prayer that I had sent up on that God awful night. My mind was made up, I wasn't going to tell them just yet. Besides, I didn't want to hit them with something like that after not seeing them for a while.

I pulled up to the house and before I could shut the car off, I could hear her voice in the distance. She was talking to her sister on the phone as if she was standing down the block. To this day I can't understand why they yell into the phone to one another. I looked up and as always, my dad was sitting on the porch. He waved like always and I trotted up the stairs to greet him. After chatting with the old man for a while, I walked up, opened the door and stepped inside the house. She looked up startled then produced a huge smile. "Wait girl, yeah, I know but you're just gonna have to hold on to that thought!" she yelled into the phone handset. "I gotta go, Bobby just stepped in so I'll call you back later," she continued. She reached over and placed the handset of the phone on its base then placed both of her hands on her knees. "Well looks like the prodigal son has finally returned."

"Hey Ma," I said cheerfully.

"Don't you 'Hey Ma' me, where have you been? Haven't seen or heard from you in more time than you're allowed. And get over here and give your mother a hug. Oh, now you think you're too cute to give your mother a hug? Boy you'd better get over here!" she said chuckling.

I rushed over to her and gave her a big hug. She kissed my face then eased over to her favorite chair and sat. "Whew, your Aunt Mary sure can talk. She's talked me silly. So, you finally decided to come see how we're doin' huh?" she asked.

"I know I've been missing from action Ma, but I've been pretty tied up. You know, work and all."

"Work? There's no job more important than your mama, remember that."

"I know, I know," I said smiling.

Just then my mother began looking at me strangely. I could see it in her eyes, it was the bloodhound coming out. "Wait, no there's something else going on," she said while squinting her eyes and pointing her finger at me.

"No, no, nothing else happening with me," I said cheerfully.

"Oh no, there's something... C'mon, what's eatin' at you? I've known you all your life son and I know when there's something bothering you. So, what's going on?"

"Nothing Ma, everything's good, I've just been working a lot and I'm probably just tired."

"Now you can go tell that mess to somebody who doesn't know you but your mama, she knows when something is eatin' at you."

"No, it's nothing really," I replied in a convincing tone.

"Well this won't cheer you up any either then. Guess you haven't heard that Sonny passed on huh?"

"Michelle's Uncle?"

"Yep, the one and only. Seems he had a massive heart attack, dropped dead at his shop."

"Wow, no I didn't know," I mumbled.

"Yeah, Michelle came by looking for you to tell you. I told her that I'd let you know. She asked me for your phone number and your address too, but I didn't give it to her."

"Why not?"

"Well I figured if you wanted her to have it, you would've given it to her yourself already."

I know this sounds terrible but, the news of Uncle Sonny's death actually did cheer me up. I knew that his death had brought Michelle back home. *Alright there you go again, judging me. How about you just keep on reading, with your self-righteous ass. Now, where was I? Oh yeah, Michelle.* Don't get me wrong, I wasn't happy that her uncle was gone, I was just happy knowing that I was going to see her again.

I hung around and visited with my parents for only a little while before heading back home. I had to change. I wanted to look my best for her. I couldn't wait to see her. Although I knew her situation, it didn't change the way I felt about her. And for something like this, the passing of one of her relatives, I'm sure he's with her.

After returning home I immediately went to work repairing and preparing myself to see Michelle. After a quick shower and shave, I ran the iron over one of my favorite shirts and slipped on a pair of jeans. I sprayed on a little cologne and rushed out of the door. As I walked to the car I could hear her calling me in the distance. It was Karen. I looked back toward her building and waved. "Bobby, got a second?" she yelled.

"It's not a good time right now, can we talk later?"

"Sure," she responded then quickly slammed the window shut.

I knew that she thought that I was blowing her off and I was. I didn't want to talk about the baby, not now. I was about to see Michelle and I didn't want to have whatever Karen had to say bring me down or upset me any more than I already was. Karen was hurt but at the moment I didn't care. For a brief second, I felt a tiny bit of compassion but it quickly crumbled up and fell to the floor. I turned the key to the ignition and pulled off.

I quickly darted though traffic and arrived at Michelle's mom's house in about twenty minutes. I walked up to the door and paused. I was about to meet her husband, the man I wanted to be. I didn't know how I would handle this but I was willing to do anything necessary to see her, to comfort her and to let her know that I still had deep feelings for her. I stood there for several seconds before the door opened. I looked up and there standing before me was a very tall, well-dressed man. My heart sank deeper and deeper with each detail that my own mind pointed out to me. He was taller, better dressed, better looking and appeared very well off based on the Rolex that hung from his wrist. He opened the glass storm door and extended his hand while speaking in a very deep voice. "How ya doing man, I'm Derric, come on in."

I stretched my arm out and we shook hands. He actually seemed like a nice guy. "The family is downstairs," he continued in his James Earl Jones sounding voice.

"Oh ok, thanks," I said now trying to add a little bass to my own voice.

"You were a friend of Sonny's?" he asked.

"*Not really, I'm just in love with your wife and I'm really just here to see her and to make sure that she's alright,*" is what I said in my mind. "Yeah, I've known him since I was a kid," I replied.

"Wow, so you and Michelle grew up together huh?"

"Yeah, I believe my pecker was the first one that she's ever seen or had laid against her skin." I replied again speaking through my mind.

"Yep," I replied.

Derric escorted me to the entrance leading to the basement. I made my down the stairs to large group of people talking, and eating. I scanned the room looking for Michelle but she was nowhere to be found. I didn't know anyone in the room so I eased over to an empty chair in the corner and sat. There was a table full of food and cake that people had brought over. I was a bit hungry and thought that a slice of that chocolate cake would keep me occupied until Michelle's return. I rose from the seat and headed over to the table and picked up a small cardboard plate. As I sliced through the deep chocolate, I could feel the warmth of her breath against my earlobe.

"Still have that sweet tooth, huh?"

I knew that voice. The entire room became completely empty. At least that's how it seemed once I turned and saw her face. It was her, my Michelle. My Michelle with the muscular, tall, deep voiced, huge hand having husband upstairs Michelle. Although I knew I could never have her, just looking at her took my breath away. I smiled and responded as clever as I could.

"You know me better than anybody else so you know if I see something sweet, I just have to at least taste it."

She looked at me as if to say, "You naughty boy."

I placed the cake on the plate and poured a cup of punch. We stood at that table and talked for about an hour and not one word about her dearly departed uncle or her huge, good looking husband upstairs was mentioned. Before you say it, I will. "That's terrible!" Hey, my hypocrisy has no bounds, what can I tell you? If it were up to me, I would've taken her upstairs and showed it to her again. What, is that wrong? I'm talking about love here, what do you know?!

Anyway, after our lengthy conversation it finally passed through my lips, the first words that I had planned to say to her when I first laid eyes on her today. "I am so sorry for your loss."

She looked deep into my eyes and replied softly, "Thank you so much Bobby and thank you for coming although I somehow knew that you would."

"You know I had to come check on my girl," I said smiling.

"I stopped by your parents' house so you'd you know that I was in town."

"Yeah, my mom said that you came by. She didn't mention Derric though," I snidely said.

"Derric, why would she mention him?" she said with a puzzled look on her face.

"I don't know. I guess I figured you would have stopped by with him so that she could have met him."

"He just got here yesterday."

"Oh, I see. He's a very lucky man."

"Oh, you've met him huh?" she asked smiling.

"Yeah, he let me in. We had a chance to get acquainted a little."

"Yeah he likes to talk and brag but rightfully so. Lucky! No, luck has nothing to do with it. He's put in the work to get what he's got," she said boastfully.

"You never seemed like the typed to be impressed by what somebody has. And putting in work, let's not get me started on that!"

"You seem to be doing pretty well for yourself Bobby."

"Just not as well as Derric, huh?" I angrily responded.

"Well unless you have your own condo in Manhattan, a place in Paris and are a partner in one of the most prestigious law firms in New York then there's a lot about you that I don't know," she said smiling.

"Wait, New York? I thought you guys lived in Atlanta."

"I do but he lives in New York."

"Well when do you guys ever see each other?"

"Mostly at family reunions once a year," she said nonchalantly.

"Hold on! At family reunions? You only see your husband at family reunions, that's crazy!"

"My husband!? No silly, oh you think... You think Derric is my husband!?" she asked as she produced a huge smile.

"Well he... I mean, the door... He said..."

"He said what? I know he didn't tell you that he was my husband. Derric is my cousin, silly."

Michelle broke out into a loud roar of laughter. I couldn't help but to laugh too. We stood there laughing uncontrollably for about ten minutes then she walked over and gave me the biggest hug. I placed my hands on her shoulders and revved back.

"Wait, If Derric's not your husband, which one of these lucky guys is?" I asked now looking around the room.

"He's not here," she responded then retreated over to the end of the table.

"What do you mean, he's not here?"

"He's not here!"

"What, he had pressing business back home or something?" I asked as I inched closer to her.

"No, it's complicated."

"Oh, ok."

"It's just... we're just trying to work some things out, that's all."

"Michelle, he should be here. Working things out is no reason not to be here when you need him most."

"I asked him not to come. We're... we're separated."

"Oh, I'm sorry. I shouldn't have... I should've minded my own business," I said while doing back flips in my mind.

She looked into my eyes and inched even closer to me, "Since when have I not been your business Bobby? You actually think that I didn't know how you felt before you said something at your apartment? I knew then like I know now. The truth of it is, we're in the process of getting a divorce. He likes his women and his drinking. I like church, movies and simple fun. I guess we both got tired of trying to convince each other to cross over to different paths."

"Michelle, I'm so sorry," I said really trying to sound sincere.

"No, you're not," she said smiling. "Why would you be?"

I had no answer for her.

"So, what's next for you?" I inquired.

"Well technically, this house is still mine. I was renting it to my uncle after my mother's passing. So, I'm going to look for a job up here and if I can find one I'm going to head back this way and live in the house."

I instantly started looking for a large piece of cardboard to throw on the floor because I was definitely going to break dance after hearing this news. I couldn't stop smiling. Just as I felt as if I was about to implode from excitement, Derric walked down the stairs and over to Michelle.

"Michelle, Aunt Darlene is on the phone and she wants to talk to you," he said.

I looked at him and rushed over and embraced him. I stepped back. He looked at me strangely and Michelle and I once again burst in laughter.

"I'll tell you later," she said while shaking her head.

I gave Michelle a hug and a kiss on the cheek then walked her upstairs. She picked up the phone receiver and we both waved goodbye. I grinned from ear to ear as I walked to my car and as I drove home.

View From My Rear Window

Chapter 12 - Sealing the Deal

I attended Uncle Sonny's funeral along with my mother. Dad remained on the front porch. Michelle stood and gave a very touching tribute to her uncle. Some I heard but of course, I was mostly focused on her. She broke down for only a brief moment and I wanted so badly to jump out of my seat and rush by her side just to comfort her. She looked at me as she concluded her tribute.

"Why wait until it's too late to tell someone that you love them. If you love them let them know now. Now, while they're here with you. Now, while you can see them smiling. Now, while you can touch them and they can touch you back. We all know that life is a short journey. Wouldn't it be nicer taking this journey with someone you love walking with hand in hand?" She continued but after she spoke those words while looking directly into my eyes I heard nothing else. Finally! It appears that we will continue what we started so many years ago.

After the services were over we returned to the house. Once again, the aroma of a multitude of fine dishes flowed through the entire house. There were people throughout the small dwelling. Seating was very limited but I did manage to find a seat for my mother. Shortly after I had retrieved a cold refreshment for my mother, Michelle walked over. She had now changed from the dark long dress and sheer dark stockings that she wore at the service to an almost quite sexy printed dress minus the nylon stockings. This caught my attention immediately because I've always admired how pretty her legs were. My mother reached for her hand but did not rise. She took Michelle by the hand and spoke to her in a sweet calm voice. "God bless you child. I know things seem difficult at this particular moment but God always makes a way."

Michelle nodded then returned her gaze in my direction. She stepped toward me and we embraced. Then she did the unexpected. She raised her head from my shoulder and very gently pressed her lips against mine. Now you know I wanted to slide my tongue softly in her mouth then kiss her savagely but it would have been somewhat inappropriate don't you think? Not that I care what you think, I'm telling this story.

With her body still pressed against mine I could begin feeling the coals heat up in the furnace. I stepped back and snatched the half-filled cup from my mother's hand just as she was raising it toward her lips to sip from it.

"I'll get you a refill," I yelled as I rushed off.

"But, I'm..." my mother muttered with her arm still extended. The faster I walked the harder I was getting. Her lips were so soft and sweet tasting.

By the time I got to the table of soft drinks I was toting half wood. I positioned myself on the other side of the table and directly in front of the punch bowl and downed the cup of punch. I began dipping the ladle into the fruity drink when up walks Michelle. "Did I say something wrong?" she asked apologetically.

"Oh no, I just know how thirsty Mom gets on days like this."

"But she hadn't even finished her drink."

"Oh, she wasn't finished?" I asked surprisingly.

"C'mon Bobby, this is me, what's wrong, what did I do?"

"You didn't do anything!"

"It was the kiss, wasn't it? And in front of your mom. I upset you, didn't I?"

"Girl, you upset me alright but not in the way you're thinking."

"You mean, you got excited from that little peck?" she asked snickering.

"Baby, you just don't know how I feel about you; how I've always felt about you since we were kids."

"Bobby, I know. I've always known. You've always shown it. Wow, I never had that effect on my husband or any other man so maybe that's a sign. I wanted to kiss you. I have for a long time but I knew it wouldn't be right. I didn't want to start anything that could lead to hurting you. You've always been special to me Bobby. You were my very first love, did you know that?"

"I don't know about your first but I do plan on being your last," I said smirking.

At that moment, Michelle and I sealed the deal. We were now finally together. I reached over the punch bowl and took both her hands in mine then whispered, "This is something that I've wanted for a very long time."

"Me too. I thought you had moved on and with my career in Atlanta, I didn't think that a long-distance relationship would work for either of us."

"Maybe we should go somewhere and seal this with a real kiss," I said then slowly licked my lips sensuously.

"Yes! Well we definitely couldn't do that here."

"Yeah, too many people huh?"

"No, you might get even more heated after that and might put somebody's eye out with that thing," she said laughing.

I too began laughing. I walked from behind the table and took her in my arms. As we headed for the door, I placed the empty cup that I had forgot to refill gently into my mother's hand as we passed by her.

"Oh, hell no! What am I supposed to do with this?" she grunted.

As we neared the front door Michelle yelled over to Derric, "We'll be right back, I just need to get some air for a minute."

Derric nodded in agreement.

I opened the door for Michelle and she crawled inside the car. I slammed the door and rushed around to the driver's side where she had already reached over and unlatched and pushed the door opened. I climbed inside still smiling. I was happier than a whore at an all-male sex anonymous meeting. *Why are YOU smiling? I know, you hate going to those damn meetings, don't you? Sorry, I digress.*

I quickly started the car and we sped off.

"We can't be too long because people will be looking to see me," Michelle said while looking behind her at the house.

"We won't. I promise. Besides, I can't leave my mother sitting there all night, she'll talk those poor folks to death," I said laughing loudly.

We rode out of the city talking and laughing. We both brought up old occurrences when we were kids and yes, we joked about our appointments. I told her everything. I told her how jealous I was when she started dating Fred and about the time when I vomited in class, was heading home and he was leaving out from giving her the ole "poke and stab." She immediately revved back in her seat after hearing this.

"The ole 'poke and stab' what is that?" she asked.

"You know, the one eyed trouser trout, the skin lizard, the poke and scream, the bump and grind, the ole slide and jerk, you know, sex!" I said laughing.

"Fred has NEVER done any of those things to me, no trouts, lizards, pokes, bumps, grinds or jerks happened over here with him! Now he did come close a couple of times but I was scared."

"Scared, why?" I asked looking surprised.

"Well you know he was on the football, baseball and basketball teams at school."

"Yeah, I know, how could I forget. Everybody laughed about how you now had a man in the ninth grade and I was still in the sixth."

We laughed for a second then she continued. "Since he played sports so much, he was kinda rough. He wasn't gentle like you and besides, you taught me how to kiss and he had no clue. He would press his lips against mine so hard and try to jam his slobbery tongue down my throat..."

"Alright, enough! I don't care if it was nine hundred years ago, I don't want to hear about that, yuck!" I said frowning.

"But you were so gentle and would touch me so tenderly like you cared. You were the one that made me feel special and you were only twelve years old. I can only imagine how it would be now."

"Well to be honest, inside my mind I loved you and as a twelve-year-old boy, all that I wanted... was to give you my one eyed trouser trout, my skin lizard, my twig and two berries..."

"Alright, I get it!" she said laughing.

We laughed a little longer then she hit me where it really hurt.

"Yep, you tried. My thighs would be raw for a week. You couldn't find that thing with a compass. We thought we were doing something too. I would lay there and you would just be going like you were getting paid by the minute. And you loved pulling that thing out too. It always smelled like 'Brylcreem' or 'Ultra Sheen', some kind of hair grease. Do you remember Brylcreem back in the day?"

"Yeah, I remember that commercial... *Brylcreem, a little dab'll do ya.*"

"Yeah, that's it! Well you must've used a big dab on that thing of yours. A twig and two berries, I think not. Even at twelve, that thing was pretty big! Well, it did have that scarf wrapped around its head and somewhat resembled one of those aardvark things but was still pretty impressive in size."

Again, with the laughter. She remembered me being uncircumcised, how embarrassed was I. I didn't laugh. I continued driving and watching the road.

<u>Chapter 13 - At Fingers Reach</u>

Michelle continued talking and laughing about the good ole days and I listened, smiled occasionally and drove. Finally, we were there. Her eyes lit up as she sat up in her seat. "This is perfect! See, you always know."

I pulled into the parking space and shut off the engine. I looked at her smiling, "The usual?" I asked. With a smile as big as the ocean, she nodded. I climbed out of the car and ran inside the small hut sized building. Five minutes later I returned to the car with two vanilla ice cream cones and napkins. Uncle Sonny used to bring a bunch of us kids up here to this very place occasionally. He would buy us all ice cream cones and take us up to his favorite spot. His spot that we later found out where he would take a lot of the older girls his age to park. I guess you know what that means and no, not a driving lesson on how to park.

This was a place of beauty. It was called "Fingers Reach." They called it that because it had the appearance of a huge lake from the distance but when you drove up to the top of the overlook, wow! If you climbed in the back seat just like we did when we were kids and looked out onto its beauty, it appeared as if you could touch every huge rock that sat in its waters with the tip of your finger. We would ride up to the top and eat ice cream and take pictures and pretend that we were sitting our cones on top of one of the huge rocks. We had so much fun there. I thought it would be appropriate since Sonny was the first to take us there.

I started the car and we headed up the winding dirt road until we reached the top. Michelle was just as excited as she used to be as a kid.

"I haven't been up here in years," she exclaimed after taking a huge lick of her cone.

"Me either."

"This reminds me of some of the best days of my life."

"I know, I feel the same way. Technically, this was probably our first date, right here."

"Yeah, that's true. We all walked up to the movie theater a few times but that was after we had been here several times," she blurted while still licking from the warming ice cream.

"Yep, and look right there. Remember?" I was pointing to an old, leaning maple tree. Michelle looked puzzled.

"No, I don't," she said shaking her head.

"You don't remember me kissing you on your cheek behind that tree? Uncle Sonny was listening to the radio and downing his beer and I leaned over and kissed your cheek. It was our first kiss actually."

"Oh yeah, I do. I remember thinking that if Uncle Sonny had seen you, he would have thrown you over the edge and dove into the lake and drowned you."

"Damn! Thank goodness he loved his beer," I said laughing.

We sat there and talked for the longest time. It felt so good being with her. It was if I didn't have a trouble in the world. We listened to soft soothing music and looked out over the beautiful lake. Most of the cars had left now, it was dusk. "You think we ought to be heading back? I'm sure people are asking about you and I'm sure that my mother's lips are extremely dry from all of the conversation that she's delivered?" I asked.

"Yeah, I guess. It's just so beautiful out here and being here with you like this brings back so many memories, good memories. I feel like a young girl again."

"Would you like for me to pull it out and rub your thigh raw to make it complete?" I asked jokingly.

"No, but you could come over here and remind me of what a good kisser you are," she said laying back against the car door.

"That would be my pleasure."

I still couldn't believe it. I was here, with the woman of my dreams and about to kiss her. Once again, coals were being thrown in the furnace and that fire was really beginning to heat up. I leaned over and placed my lips on hers. They were so soft. She gently opened her mouth and I slowly slid my tongue into the warm opening. It was almost heavenly. I say almost because I'm not quite sure what heaven is like. It now felt as if the little worker down there said to hell with the coal and just started pouring gasoline on the fire. I was raging inside but knew that I had to get her back home. I placed my arm on the back of the seat to pull myself up. What she did next, I'll never forget. Michelle place her hand on the back of my neck and pulled me back to her. She began kissing me harder and breathing as if she had just run a marathon. She reached down and placed her hand in the "Fire Zone." As you already know, I didn't need much of an excuse to go for it. I laid between her legs and her eyes opened wide as she felt the new and improved me. We carried on for several minutes and once again I pulled myself off of her.

"We'd better get back, baby." Believe me, it was just as hard for me to say that as it is for you believe it. I sat up and leaned over to open the door. Michelle lifted her left leg and placed it on top of the seat. She pulled her dress up higher, then with her other hand slid the crotch part of her panties over to one side.

"You sure you just don't want to touch it once before we go?" she asked while looking at me inviting me in.

I looked around and all the other cars were gone; all but one and the windows of that car were so steamy that I couldn't see inside. I looked at Michelle in all her splendor. I remember thinking... *"This girl's a ho! After all this time of wanting and waiting for her, she's just a hot ass ho!"* Then I thought... *"Hoes are good... Every woman needs a little ho in 'em."* and I continued on.

I couldn't wait to show it to her. Now circumcised and better than ever before, she looked and admired it. The only thing else that was missing was, my father's hair grease. She raised herself up and took hold of me. I watched on as she inched her face near to its one eye. What she did next left me speechless. Her tongue wrapped and slid in ways unimaginable. She was drawing my excitement to a premature blast. I stopped her to collect myself. I wanted her and not just that way. After regrouping, I laid on top of her and just to be funny I poked it right on the side of her thigh.

"Remember that?" I asked laughing.

She reached down and positioned it then replied, "Let's get it right this time."

We too, steamed up the windows of the car and tested the shocks of that vehicle for over an hour. By the time we climbed back into the front seats, my knees were raw and she had a crick in her neck. We were both sweaty but both truly satisfied.

"If I had known that you could work it like that, I would have still been with you now, even if you were still in the sixth grade," Michelle said chuckling and trying to fix her hair.

"I knew you were going to be everything that I expected. I'm really glad this happened."

"Me too and I hope that it happens again and again and again and again..." she said laughing.

"It can, it will."

"I don't know what it is but it's just something about doing it outside. Maybe it's the chance of getting caught, I don't know. Next time, let's bring a blanket and get out of the car and do it."

"Uh, ok. That is if no other cars are up here," I replied then returned to my "ho" thoughts.

"I can't wait for the next time."

"In that case, can I see you tomorrow?"

"You can see me every day if you want. I've waited for something like this all my life. Somebody that I know really cares about me and who really loves me."

"I do and I always have Michelle."

I started the car and headed back down the hill for home. I smiled while thinking of what we had just done. We arrived at the house thirty minutes later. Michelle was welcomed by new visitors as soon as she walked inside the door and the ladies sitting, talking with my mother looked to me for rescuing. I collected my mother and took her home before heading home myself.

After only a few passing days, Michelle was heading back to Atlanta. We had spent every day together. She would come over to my place and we would make love all day until we were light headed or starving. She loved it. I'm telling you, she couldn't get enough! But I was willing to keep giving her an injection every time she was in need or in want. It hurt me to know that she was going back home to him. Even though it was over, there was so much stress and pain that she still had to deal with back home.

<u>Chapter 14 - TRUTH</u>

Michelle and I communicated by phone daily. We talked about our future and even about kids. That was still a thorn in my side. I still hadn't confessed my future offspring to her yet. Things were going so great that I didn't want anything to trouble it. So many thoughts ran through my mind concerning my situation. I didn't want to spring this on her, not yet. She was going through enough already.

Several days had passed and Michelle and I continued our normal routine. I missed her but knew that she would be back soon enough. I was making preparations for her return already. I knew that I was going to have to deal with Karen. Michelle would be back soon and it would only be a matter of time before they were face to face. I also knew that it would be a slap in the face to her once she realized that Michelle was not actually my wife nor living with me. Now thoughts of child support hearings and arguments rained through my head.

"Damn, you see what kind of trouble you got me into?" I yelled out loud while tugging at my crotch.

Yep, this was going to have to be played very carefully. I flopped down on the sofa and looked up at the ceiling letting out the longest sigh. My stressing was soon interrupted by a ringing telephone. I pulled myself up and walked over and answered. "Hello."

"Hey Baby!" It was her, it was Michelle.

"Hey yourself!"

"What are you up to? You're not up there cheating on me, already are you?" she asked jokingly.

"Well, hookers don't count, do they?"

"I guess not since you have to pay them."

"In that case, that'll be a no," I said laughing.

We talked for several minutes then she hit me with it.

"So, baby, it looks like I've found a job up there. I sent my resume to a couple of law firms there and I've already had two phone interviews and I'm scheduled for a face-to-face in a couple of weeks."

"So, you'll be back that soon?" I asked while trying to contain my excitement.

"Soon enough baby. There is one glitch though."

"What's that?"

"Well Steven... He's been harassing me and stalking me. I had to put out a restraining order on him because he won't leave me alone. He said that he would never let me leave. We were trying to share the house until he..."

"He what?" I asked sternly.

"Well..."

"Tell me! What did he do?!"

"We were sleeping in separate rooms and the other night... the other night he came into the room and tried forcing himself on me. I told him no but he kept grabbing and pulling on me and yelling how I was still his wife. I fought him off as much as I could until..."

"What? Until what?" I mumbled angrily.

"He took me."

After her words, you could cut through the silence with a knife. I could feel the rage inside of me growing by the second. I couldn't speak. I just stood there. I know what you're thinking. It's his damn wife, how in the hell could I possibly be angry? Or, you might be thinking... now how did her dumb ass think that was going to play out if he still wanted her, right? The same thoughts ran through my mind as well but I was still angry knowing that this man had just taken some of what I now considered mine! I was furious.

Finally, she broke the silence with even more bad news.

"He also said that if I move back there he was coming too," she continued.

"Coming here, for what?"

"To be with me. He said that he's never going to let me leave him and if I try he'll kill me because he'd rather see me dead than to see me with anybody else."

"Oh, this fool is crazy! How did you get mixed up with a lunatic like that?" I asked.

"He wasn't like that when I met him."

"Well he's like that now. What set him off, did you tell him about us?"

"No, he would come after you and I don't want that."

"Well what did the police say?'

"They told me to file a restraining order which I did. The judge said that he could be arrested if he comes within one hundred feet of me."

"So, then you're still coming, right?"

"Yes. I'll be there in a couple of weeks."

"Ok, you be careful down there and keep me posted as to what's going on with him."

"I will," she said sweetly.

Michelle and I ended our conversation for the evening. I went back to the couch and contemplated the possible outcome from all of this.

The following morning I set out for the grocery store. It was Saturday and a nice day. I could feel the strong heat from the sun penetrating the thin cotton of my sweat shirt. I stopped on the stoop for a brief second and looked around the parking lot before heading for my car. I walked over to my vehicle and inserted my key into the door lock. Just as I turned the key I could see the dark silhouette from the corner of my eye. It was magnificent. The curves of that body were as if someone had drawn a picture of the most perfect figure and placed it on the concrete pavement. I slowly turned my head to get a full view of this goddess. Standing there with her arms folded was Karen. Man,

I forgot just how built she really was. She inched closer to the car before speaking to me.

"So, are you gonna finally sit down and talk to me? We need to seriously talk Bobby."

I pulled my key from the door lock and stepped up onto the curb. "I know, I know we do."

"So, is now not a good time?"

"Well Karen, I do have to run out for a while, how about as soon as I get back?"

"No Bobby, we need to talk now!" she said now raising her voice.

She was right, we did need to discuss what we were going to do. I slid my keys back into my pants pocket and extend my hand directing her to the stairs leading back into the building. Once inside the apartment, Karen walked over and flopped down on the couch and immediately started in on me. This was a different Karen; a Karen I had never seen before.

"So, Bobby, have you even given this any thought?" she asked

"Yes, I mean... sure."

"So what are we going to do? I already have three kids, I can't raise four on my own and if you're even thinking about me having an abortion... forget about it! This baby is going to live. So again, I ask you, what are we going to do?"

"Look, I don't know what you want me to tell you. You've already decided for the both of us that you're keeping the baby. So, I guess the only thing I can say is that I'll support my child. I'll be there for it too."

"It? You refer to our child as an it?"

"Well he or she, is that better?"

Karen turned up her lips and looked away from me displaying her disgust. I had no idea how to convince her to not have this baby. Michelle was not going to take this news lightly I was sure. Now that Michelle was in my life there was no room or need for Karen but now as it seems, I'm stuck with her.

Karen went on telling me what I needed to do as a man and how hard she could make it for me if I didn't as she put it, "step up." I reassured her over and over that I would and how we both were responsible. She didn't want to hear that. She just wanted to be angry for some reason. I was sitting there agreeing with her and telling her everything that I thought that she wanted to hear. The conversation just wasn't going well at all. I couldn't understand why she was so angry that is, until she started asking me about our future. Karen finally stood up. I was hoping that she had finally gotten all of her answers and was about to leave. She walked up to me and placed both of hands on my chest. "So, what about us? Don't you think we would be good together? We've been seeing each other all this time and it's been so good, why stop?"

I placed my hands on both her wrists and slid them down to her side. I looked her directly in her big brown eyes and lied. "Because I have a wife."

Karen stepped back. I could tell her mind was racing for a response. She looked down at the floor then folded her arms once again and raised her head abruptly. "No you don't!" she yelled.

"No I don't what?"

"No you don't have a wife that's what," she continued yelling.

I stood quiet and motionless for a second wondering what or how she knew. Maybe she was just taking a stab in the dark hoping to get a confession out of me. Never the less, I wasn't going to break from her attempt.

"I don't know what makes you think that," I replied sternly.

"That is the biggest untruth that I have ever heard pierce your lips."

"Karen, I have a wife, Michelle."

"So you have a wife named Michelle, who's in the military overseas huh?" she asked while placing her hands on her hips.

"That's right, if you don't believe me, she'll be here in a couple of weeks and you can see for yourself. I've been trying to figure out how I'm going to tell her about the baby. That's why it took me so long to get back to you."

"Uh huh. Well the last time I checked, Atlanta Georgia was in the United States!"

Damn, I was busted! That explained why she was so pissed. She knew the entire time. Alright, I had to think and fast. I walked into the dining room and sat down in the chair furthest away from her. I calmly spoke. "You're right, we're not legally married but more like common law."

"That's bull Bobby, you've never lived with that woman a day in your life so how is that common law?"

Wow, this woman has done her homework and I don't know what or who her reference was. Once again, I collected myself from yet another gut punch that Karen had delivered. I decided on another approach. She was already angry so I guess the truth is just as good as anything else I could come up with at this juncture. I tried again. "She's someone that I've been seeing for a very long time."

Ok, I wasn't quite ready to go with the truth thing just yet. Karen stormed over to me an opened both barrels. The onslaught left me weak and speechless. As she pointed her finger in my face she lashed out.

"Seen her for a long time my ass! That woman would barely give you the time of day. You've been running around chasing her and sniffing her ass before you could even piss straight. You've had a pathetic infatuation with this woman since forever and she still doesn't want you. All these years, she's been sleeping with everybody with a swinging dick but you and you can't see it. I'm standing right here, right now. A woman who loves you for who you are, not who you used to be. A woman that will always love you that you will never have to chase. A woman who will take care of you and will be there for you no matter what. Why wouldn't you want to be with this woman?"

"Because I don't love you. I love her."

"What about all we have?" she shouted.

"All what? We don't have anything. We've never had anything. Nothing but sex and look where that's gotten us."

Karen became even more furious than she was.

"You're a twisted man Bobby," she barked.

"I'm just in love with somebody else Karen, I'm sorry."

"You're not sorry! You're living a lie in your mind and everybody in your old neighborhood knows and are laughing at you. You view her as a saint when she's nothing but the devil."

"You don't know her!" I yelled furiously.

"No but Fran does. That's right, Fran. Fran Washington who lived just three doors down from where your precious Michelle lived. We used to work together and I recently ran into her at the mall. I told her that I was pregnant again and she asked who the father was. When I mentioned your name, she told me that she knew you and had grown up in the same neighborhood as you and her dad still lived there. She blabbed all of your business. Told me that you have never been married and about your parents. Told it all and said that she hoped I could straighten you out but I see that I can't. Only a Psychiatrist can straighten your crazy ass out because you are in desperate need of some serious couch time. But you know what, you keep chasing your ghost girlfriend and see where THAT gets you. Just know, even though you're confused, I will always love you Bobby."

Karen turned and stormed out the door.

Chapter 15 - Admissions of Candor

The weeks passed quickly. I had no more contact with Karen as she was still quite angry and hurt with me. This was the day that Michelle was returning. She was to meet me at my parents' house after she had arrived and gotten settled in. After showering and getting dressed, I sprayed on the spicy fragrance that Michelle loved and hurried out the door. I drove over to the old neighborhood and stopped in to see my folks. My dad was sitting on the front porch. He waved as I got out of the car. "Hey son," he yelled.

"What's going on Pop?"

"Nothing much, just taking in a little air is all."

"Where's Ma?"

"You know where, in the kitchen yapping on the phone with your aunt Mary."

"Don't they ever get tired? I mean really, how much can they have to talk about."

"I believe when they run out of things to talk about, they just start making things up," he said while chuckling.

"Let me go say hello."

My dad reached over and pulled the screen door open. I place my hand on his shoulder and entered the house. My mother was right where he said she'd be and doing exactly what we both knew she'd be doing. She motioned me to come over and gave me a hug from her seated position. She did what she usually would do when I came over, told my aunt that she would call her back. She hung the phone up and asked where my dad was. I sat down at the table directly across from her and we talked for a while. She would always ask the same questions. She'd ask about my job, my bills and of course my love life and I always had the same answers for the most part but not today. Of course when she brought up my love life, I told her about Michelle returning and us being together. Shockingly to me, she didn't seem pleased. She reached up and took off her eyeglasses which always was the indication of a lecture.

"That Michelle sure is a sweet girl," she started.

"Yeah, she is," I added.

"I used to talk to her mother a lot before she passed. She was a sweet woman too."

"Oh yeah, I really liked Mrs. Taylor."

"You know, I remember being outside hanging up my laundry when she came strolling by, Mrs. Taylor that is. She stopped at the fence and we gotta talkin' about a little bit of everything. Woooo that woman could talk too."

My mother would say the same thing about every woman that she talked to with the exception of herself. She picked up the small cloth that lay beside her tea cup and began wiping the lenses of her eyewear as she continued. "Oh yeah, we talked about our kids and everybody else's kids that played with ours. I remember talking about the little girl next door and how she and Michelle were such good friends and all. Then she told me how she had to run her out of her house one day because she and Michelle well you know."

"I know what?" I asked looking as if I had no clue of what she was talking about.

"You know, she caught them doing the lesbian thing. She said it was the nastiest thing that she had ever laid eyes on. And of course, she said that the girl was making Michelle do it because Michelle was afraid of the girl. I think that's a bunch of bull hockey myself. Just when you think you know somebody, you find out that you don't really know them at all."

"Oh well I know Michelle pretty well and I'm sure that was just two little girls experimenting with their bodies and nothing more."

"Well to tell you the truth I don't think that they were all that young," my mother said while sliding her glasses back onto her face.

"C'mon Ma, surely you don't..."

Just then we both heard the door open and Dad telling someone to go right on in. It was Michelle. She walked into the house and greeted my mother. I stood up and as I walked past my mother she mumbled, "We'll finish this conversation later."

I looked down at her then back at Michelle. I walked up and gave her a tight huge and then we both sat down on the couch. My dad entered the house and my mother stood up.

"Let me get you something to drink child," she said. "I've got tea, water and even some ginger ale and cola if you want," she continued.

"Oh no ma'am, no thank you, I'm fine," Michelle replied.

We all sat and talked for over an hour before Michelle and I headed back to my place stripped and did what we both loved doing. We promised my mom that we would return and have dinner with them so we weren't wasting any time.

After completing our mission, we lay there quietly. She was laying on her stomach and I was caressing her back. She had the prettiest skin. Michelle rolled over on her side and looked at me strangely.

"What's wrong?" I asked.

She looked down at the bed then began to speak. "Bobby, maybe we should stop seeing each other until I get everything straight. I mean the divorce and make sure that Steven is not going to do anything crazy."

"Aww, he's not going to do anything, he was just trying to scare you into staying with him is all."

"No Bobby, he is mentally unstable. I don't know what he might do and I'd rather be safe than sorry. I love you Bobby but not enough to put you in harm's way. So I'm not asking you, I'm telling you, I don't want to see you until I have everything under control."

All I could do was look at her in disbelief. All of that time of waiting and wanting her. Now I'm back waiting and wanting again. I was crushed. I rolled on my back and placed both hands behind my head. I stared at the ceiling for a while taking all of this in, then without giving it any thought at all, I blurted it out. "There's something I need to tell you as well."

"What is it?" she asked.

"Well, before we got together I was kind of seeing someone. I mean it wasn't anything serious or even a little serious. Actually, it was nothing at all..."

"It was sex, that's what it was. It's ok, I didn't think you were a choir boy for all those years Bobby. There's nothing to confess. Ok, I wasn't your first," she said smiling.

"No, there's more to it than just that. I didn't know how or..."

"Or what, just tell me," she interrupted.

"She's pregnant."

Michelle sat up in the bed and looked down at me in disbelief. I looked over at then quickly turned my eyes downward.

"Pregnant! By you?" she said in a shaky voice as if she were trying to control her anger.

"You wait until now to tell me this! You've known this the entire time that you were pursuing me!? I don't believe this. With everything that I have going on, you add this. No, no, I can't do this.

You sit and talk about kids and family to me, our family, and you bring this to me!" she continued.

Michelle jumped out of the bed and stormed around the room mumbling profanities while gathering her clothes. I too, hopped out of the bed, grabbed my jeans and struggled to put them on as quickly as I could.

"Baby, can't we talk about this?" I asked in a calm voice.

She quickly slipped on each garment and snatched her purse off the chair. As she rushed out of the room, I followed.

"C'mon now, talk to me," I said still trying to calm her down.

She acted as if she couldn't hear a word that I spoke. She rushed toward the door and quickly yanked the deadbolt to its unlocked position and flung the door open.

"Tell your mother that I won't make it for dinner!" she yelled looking back at me.

As I approached the door, she stormed out slamming the door behind her. She was hot! I opened the door and called out to her, "Michelle! Baby!" She continued down the stairs and onto the side walk then it hit me, she rode with me here. I quickly rushed back into my bedroom and snatched up my remaining garments that were tossed all over during the heat of passion. I threw them on, grabbed my wallet and keys and headed for the door. I ran out of the building and hopped into my car and sped off to catch her. As I pulled up to the entrance driveway of the complex I could see Michelle climbing into the black

and yellow cab. I sat in the driveway waiting for the traffic to subside.
As I pulled out onto the main street, I could see the transport which
stowed her racing though the intersection. I pulled up to the corner of
the busy intersection then stopped abruptly as the traffic light had now
turned red. I decided to give her some time and space then made a
quick "U" turn towards home.

Chapter 16 - With My Own Eyes

Depressed and saddened by the previous incident, I didn't feel much like going to my parents' for dinner but it was probably better than sitting in that empty apartment moping. I showered and put on some fresh clothes and headed back to the old neighborhood. As I pulled up to the front of the house, yes, you guessed it, Dad was sitting on the front porch waving. I backed into the vacant parking space directly in front of the house and turned off the ignition. I sat there for a moment collecting myself and building my "I'm ok" face for the lady detective inside. My mother could always tell when there was something wrong with me so I knew I'd better get it together before going inside.

Now situated, I balled my car keys up in my hand, popped the lock to the door and climbed out of the car. I looked up onto the porch and waved to my dad. As I stepped back to shut the car door, the car pulled up. It stopped directly across from me. My dad looked strangely at the automobile and I slowly turned towards it. The windows were tinted on the fire red 1984 mustang so I couldn't see the driver. As I turned to step away the automatic window slowly made its descent. There sitting behind the steering wheel was none other than Fred. He removed his dark shades and smiled in a pompous sort of way. "Bobby... Bobby... Bobby, my man," he said still smiling. I just looked at him. He looked back as if to check for oncoming traffic then opened his door. He stepped outside of the car and walked over to me. *"Ok, let me beat his ass right now and in front of Pop too,"* I thought. *"Yeah, as soon as he gets close enough I'm bustin' him dead in the chops."*

As Fred stepped closer, I started balling up a nice, hard fist. I was ready and wanted to pound his face in for a long time. Just when I was about to step up to bang his nose through the back of his head he stopped. "Bobby, look here man, I just wanted to stop and apologize for the silly incident we had the last time that we saw each other. It was totally uncalled for on my part and was pretty petty of me. You've always been a nice guy; a good dude and I've always been sort of a jerk I guess. I just wanted to stop and apologize," he said.

"Really?" I thought. If my dad hadn't heard him, I would've still planted my size twelve's in his hind parts but how would that look? I guess I should be cool about it. Fred extended his hand to me and I looked at it. Then from the distance I could hear my dad yell... "It takes a real man to admit when he was wrong." And with that, I reached out and shook his hand. We both stepped around the back of my car and onto sidewalk. I looked over at his car and said, "Nice car."

"Yeah, it's a real chick magnet," he replied arrogantly.

"Yeah, I can see how it could be."

"Man, that was a real mess after the funeral, huh?"

"Yeah, I guess."

"I guess I still have those old twinges around her after all these years but I'm sure you can relate huh?"

"Well not really, she seems to be taking care of those twinges that I have these days."

"Whaaat, you ole dog you! You still hittin' that?" he asked while slapping me on the back.

"Every chance I get," I replied sort of arrogantly.

"Wow! Well you know what they say... you had her your way and I had her mine," he said laughing.

"Yeah but I had her ALL the way," I said with a smug look on my face.

"What's that supposed to mean?"

"Ah c'mon Fred, she told me that you guys never did anything so you can drop the act."

"What! Is that what she told you?"

Fred began laughing uncontrollably. He placed his hand on my shoulder, bent over and placed his other hand on his stomach trying to relieve the pain from his laughter. In other words, he was cracking up! After calming himself, Fred looked up at me and asked, "You don't really believe that do you?"

"I believe it if she said it. Why would I believe you over her? Why would she lie?"

"Maybe to make you think she's some type of princess or something. Hell everybody knows that we were working it out. She was hot as fire but I'm sure you already know that. Hell, that's why she and I split up."

"Yeah, why did you two break up? Were you not satisfied with her so much that you had to chase every girl in the school who thought you were some type of God because you played sports? That's what I'm thinking."

"Heck no man. Michelle and I split because I walked in the locker room going to soak a sore hamstring and I walked into the shower area and she's up against the locker getting done by Reggie Dawson and Tyrone at the same time. I later heard after we broke up that she screwed half the basketball team, four members of the football team and heard that she even gave Mr. Wilson the old gym teacher some."

"Man, I think you'd better take your lying, filthy mouth back to your car before this gets real ugly. I'm not gonna stand here and let you talk about her like that."

"Bobby, look man, I don't mean any disrespect at all, I'm just trying to let you know firsthand, how she was."

"Well how about I don't believe your firsthand bull."

Just as our conversation was heating up, Fred leaned forward and peered down the walkway. I turned to see what or who he was looking at. "Well I'll be! Now this isn't a sight that you see every day, two roosters at the henhouse at the same time," he said as he approached laughing.

It was Donald, still my play big brother, the provider of my first piece. As he drew nearer, I turned to meet him. We embraced and slapped each other on the back. He reached over and shook Fred's hand.

"What are you guys doin', just chewing the fat?" he asked chuckling.

"Yeah, just reminiscing on old times is all," Fred said.

"Oh, in that case I can only imagine what or should I say "Who, " Donald added.

"Yeah, she was something back in the day," Fred said as he leaned back on the fence.

"Hell, she's still something today, that girl will never change," said Donald.

"Well fellas I've got to get goin', got a hot date that I've gotta get to. It was good seeing you both and Bobby, remember what I said... a leopard never changes its spots," Fred said as he headed back toward his car.

Donald and I both bid him farewell and good riddance then continued our conversation.

"What a jerk," I said.

"Don't we all know," Donald replied.

"I'd really like to kick his ass."

"He's not even worth it Lil Bro. And what in the hell was that about? A leopard, who in the hell is he supposed to be now, Zino of Citium?"

Ok, don't feel bad, I didn't know who in the hell Zino of Citium was either. Guess we both better look him up but Donald was heavy into philosophy and just about anything else that was in a book. After looking at him as puzzled as I could, I uttered the only words that my brain would allow, "Zino who?"

"Man, pick up a damn book sometime. Never mind that, who's a leopard?"

"He was trying to tell me that the only reason he and Michelle split up was because he caught her screwing around with some guy while they were together. He's just trying to make her look like a slut because he never got it that's all."

"Who never got what?"

"That jackass Fred, he never got with Michelle."

"You talkin' sexually?"

"Yeah."

"Who told you that bull?"

"It's not bull, she did."

"Man, Michelle is lying to you but that's what she does. I know that was your first little girlfriend and all and you can't see beyond that. She's something else man."

"Well why would she lie? She has no reason to lie but he does," I added to her defense.

"Well I don't. Let me tell you something, Fred had done Michelle in my house. I've seen them and heard them many times. She probably lied because she doesn't want you to have that image of her in your mind."

"I just don't believe that, not her. I don't believe him and I don't believe you."

"Lil Bro. you know I've never lied to you, not ever! The girl was out there and I'm pretty sure that she hasn't changed. As a matter of fact, I know she hasn't changed."

"Why do you say that?" I asked looking at him inquisitively.

"Look, Fred use to do Michelle at my house because my mom didn't get off from work until six o'clock. This one particular day, they were down the basement and I was in the kitchen. The couch was against the wall at the bottom of the stairs. When I walked over to the sink, I looked down the stairs and saw Fred on top of her pumping. It was dark but the light from the window provided just enough light for me to see. All of a sudden, I can see Michelle's face looking up at me. I was a little embarrassed and thought she was going to try to cover up or something. Instead, she looked me dead in the eyes and smiled. I didn't know how to take that or what to do so I smiled back. She waved her hand for me to come downstairs and Fred looked over his shoulder then asked her what was she doing. She said, 'let him join us.' Fred told her no and asked her if she was crazy. I went back upstairs. The next day, I heard a knock at the door. When I went to open the door, I could see her standing on the porch. I didn't see Fred. I opened the door and she came inside. She said nothing. She only took my hand and led me to the basement. She took off her top then unbutton my pants and..."

"Stop! Why are you doing this? Why are you making all of this crap up?" I shouted.

"Bobby, all I'm trying to tell you is that I've been with her and so have a lot of the other guys in the neighborhood. She portrays herself as this sweet wholesome girl but she's not."

"I still don't believe you," I said now holding my head in my hands.

"Look man, I can see that it's harder to convince you than it was for Thomas Aquinas to convince folk of the existence of God. I know you can't help who you love but at least know who you love. Don't be blind to the truth because it will always resurface sooner or later," Donald said in all of his infinite wisdom.

As Donald seemed to reach the end of his sermon, the front door was opened to the house and my mom stuck her head out.

"Boy come on in here and eat, we're not going to wait all evening, we're hungry. Hi there Donald, you wanna come in for some dinner?" she asked

"No ma'am, I just ate, but thanks," he replied.

My mother went back inside and Donald and I embraced once again. "Remember what I said man," he continued.

I nodded and walked through the gate. I waved to Donald and he returned in the direction from once he came.

As soon as I stepped inside the house my mother sat down at the table.

"Where's your little girlfriend? She's awfully late." she asked.

"She can't make it today."

"Oh. You two have a little spat?"

"No, she just had something that came up at the last minute."

"Uh huh..."

"Can we talk about something else please?"

My mother gave me her special look that meant that the discussion was not over. She then looked over to my dad and asked him to bless the food which he did. We ate and talked about everything but Michelle.

After dinner I hugged my folks and headed home. I wasn't home five minutes before the phone rang. I walked and over and answered it, "Hello."

"If you want to know the truth, come over to my house right now!"

It was Donald. I didn't know what was going on but it seemed that my curiosity had already gotten the best of me. I was sure he was mistaken and if anything, would prove him wrong.

I jumped in the car and headed back. On the way, I was already envisioning what he saw or thought he saw. She was upset with me and probably is going off on a date with some guy or even invited him over. What else could it be?

I arrived shortly and parked down the street from Donald's mother's. Donald no longer lived there but his mother was a lot more elderly than most of ours and he spent much of his time taking care of her. I crept down the walk and trotted up to Donald's mom's front door. Before I could knock on the door, Donald opened it.

"Come on in," he whispered.

I stepped inside looking around as if to see something that he had discovered.

"So what am I supposed to be seeing?" I asked.

Donald walked me upstairs to the rear bedroom. Ok, this was feeling a little weird. I was hoping that Michelle wasn't back there doing it with Fred based on what Donald's prior story was trying to reveal. He walked over to the window and I followed. He kept the light off, picked up a pair of binoculars that were laying on the bed and peered out for a few seconds.

"They've been going at it for a while now," he said.

He handed me the binoculars, "See for yourself."

I looked through the lenses and could see directly into Michelle's living room. I could also see two shadowy figures moving slowly on the couch. I watched on for a few more seconds then removed the huge spectacles from my eyes.

"That doesn't mean anything, that could be anybody," I said.

Just as I was about to continue my argument and return home, Michelle's living room light illuminated. Donald and I both stood peering through the window. Suddenly the porch light of her home lit up brightly. It was bright enough for us to see the entire porch. As the door opened we both leaned closer to the window but tried to remain out of view. The two bodies stepped into the exit way and we could see both of the individuals clearly.

"See, you got all excited about nothing. There's nothing going on there," I said to Donald.

He looked at me with this weird, disapproving look. I continued, "You got me all the way back over here for this? It's just her and Alli..." Just as I was about to finish scolding him the two embraced and kissed passionately. They kissed hard and long. I couldn't believe it! My mother was right. It was Michelle and Allison and they had just made love. I was devastated.

After seeing Michelle and Allison, all I could do was drag myself down the stairs and out the door. Donald and I didn't speak a word to one another. He only placed his hand on my shoulder and opened the door. I stepped outside and with my head down and body slumped over, I walked to my car. I don't even remember the ride home. I only remember laying in my bed staring at the ceiling and thinking of how much of a fool I've been. And with all that had happened... I still loved her. I know, call me a fool. I'd have to agree with you but like Donald said, you can't help who you love. I had no idea how to handle this. I didn't know if I should confront her or just learn to live with it.

Chapter 17 - The Motor Mouth

The morning seemed to come in a flash. I hadn't slept a wink. I stayed awake with thoughts racing through my mind all night. Even after the sun came up, I laid there lifeless contemplating what my next move should be. When I finally rose, I felt lightheaded and still in a daze. I walked into the bathroom and with bloodshot eyes turned on the faucet. I washed my face and brushed my teeth. Now starving and not feeling like doing anything, especially cooking, I slipped on my clothes and headed for the IHOP next to the mall.

I arrived at the restaurant at 7:35 a.m. and it was already getting crowded. I just wanted to be left alone.

"Just one?" the hostess asked.

I nodded while responding, "Yes."

"Follow me please."

The hostess led the way through the aisles to the back of the restaurant. It was perfect. I sat down and she passed me the menu and announced their specials of the day. I thanked her and she headed back to her station. Shortly after, a large shadow rose up from the side of the table then over my face. I looked up and standing over me was a large, heavyset woman toting a carafe of coffee and a mug. She walked up closer to the table, "Coffee?" she asked.

I removed my dark glasses and only nodded. She poured the hot, dark coffee into the mug and placed it before me. She sat the carafe of coffee down and pulled a short thick pad and pencil out from her apron then asked, "So what can I get you?"

"Eggs, just eggs please."

"How many would you like?"

"Three eggs over easy and two pieces of toast please."

The woman reached out and I placed the menu in her hand. She turned and rushed off. I slid my shades back onto my face and looked out onto the parking lot. Too quick for my meal to be ready, the shadow reappeared.

"Well... well... well... if it isn't Mr. Bobby, himself."

The voice spoke much too loudly to be in a public place so I knew it had to be some uncouth person that I didn't feel like dealing with this morning. It was. I turned and looked over while already thinking of excuses for them to just go away. It was Fran. Just what I needed, her loud, boisterous ass. She walked up with her big handbag cupped in the crease of her arm talking as if we were the only people in the restaurant.

"Fancy seeing you in here," she said loudly.

"You think you can tone it down a tad? I've got a huge hangover."

"Oh sorry Babe."

Without asking or me offering, Fran sat her handbag on the table and flopped down in the seat across from me. "So, what's been going on with you?" she asked.

"I think you know."

"What?"

"Don't act like you don't know. Karen, your old co-worker..."

"Oh you mean your baby's mama?" she said with a short giggle.

"Yeah Rona Barrett! So you had to go and tell her all of my business, huh?"

"No baby, she was standing there bragging on her babies like she always has. When she said that she was pregnant again and started bragging on the father I just asked who he was and if he had any brothers," she continued while giggling even more.

"Well that's not all you said," I angrily whispered.

"I know, she just pissed me off when she said it was you. I wanted to tell her so bad that I was the only woman that was going to have your baby."

Now laughing and moving her bag to the windowsill she waved the waitress over and ordered a coffee and the grand breakfast platter.

"Why did you have to get into my business with her?" I asked.

"Because I knew it would piss her off. And what do you want with that baby maker anyway, how many kids does she have already, ten? Well anyway it did piss her off too. After our little conversation, we agreed to get together for lunch the following weekend and we did. She's so pissed at you, she's going to make you suffer and ride it out."

"Suffer, ride what out? What in the hell are you talking about?"

"Well, you ain't heard this from me but there ain't no baby. She thought she was pregnant, she really did but then she had her period. But since she's so pissed, she said that she wasn't going to tell you a damn thing. Said she was gonna let you suffer for months until you finally figured it out on your own. That should be enough time to do some damage in your relationship with you know who."

"You're lying!?"

"Nope, she told me out of her own mouth. Now, she'll probably tell you that I'm lying but if you don't believe me, you'll see in about two or three months from now. The only way her stomach will get any bigger is if she keeps on eating her kids' leftover happy meals."

"I'm going make her tell me the truth!" I said while banging my fist on the table.

"Just like a man, stupid! Look, you can't go bustin' in there, shaking her and expect her to tell you the truth. Noooo, not a scorned woman oh no. You have to play it smart, you have to think like a woman. Now if it were me, I'm just saying, I'd cuddle up to her. You know, make her feel wanted. Tell her that you told Michelle that it's over and you want to be the best dad ever. Then you'll see her for who she is. With or without the kid you now see that she's always been the woman for you. You know, some crap like that. She'll come clean," she said then shrugged her shoulders.

I had to admit, Ms. Uncouth had a good idea. And if anybody knew anything about hustling somebody, it would be Fran.

"That's actually a good idea," I said nodding my head.

"Hell yeah it is, and no charge. See, aren't you glad I opened my big mouth now, cause if I hadn't, you would've been stuck with Ms. Fertile for a good while. She probably would have sexed you to death until she really was pregnant or gotten pregnant by somebody else and you wouldn't have known the difference. Women can be cruel. She just would have told you that she carried the baby longer or something crazy like that and your stupid ass would have accepted whatever she told you."

As crazy as it sounds, she was right. I told Michelle about the baby that was non-existent and she left me. I would have been with Karen splashing my seed in her without hesitation because I would have thought that she was already pregnant.

As I pondered on my strategy for Karen, the waitress walked over with our food. We sat, ate and continued talking for a while. After we were done, the waitress brought over the bill. Fran collected her things and thanked me for breakfast. She told me that she'd get me next time then hurried off. Like I said, *"If anybody knew anything about hustling somebody, it would be Fran."*

Later that evening, after finally getting some sleep, I walked over to Karen's apartment. I tapped on the door using the metal knocker. There was no answer. I knocked once again with my knuckles and waited a few seconds longer. Still, no answer. As I turned to walk down the stairs, the door slowly opened. I turned and walked up to the door and there she stood. The stern look on her face was just a reminder that she was still angry. I was angry too but knew that Fran's idea would produce the outcome that I so desperately needed. I couldn't afford to wait for months to know the truth or give her a chance to do God knows what.

"Well, are you going to ask me in?" I asked.

Karen said nothing, she just pushed the door opened, turned and walked away. I caught the door as it began to close and stepped inside. I walked up to Karen as she stood there with her arms folded. I placed my arms on her shoulders and just as I was about to speak the thunderous bumping and slamming noises caught both our attention.

"Bobby!" the high pitched squeaky voice rang out.

"Get back in that room and don't you come back out here 'til I tell you to, now go!"

It was Justin, Karen's youngest boy. He heard my voice and had come out to greet me. After I heard the door to the kids' room close I continued with my semi-rehearsed speech. I kept my hands on her shoulders and looked her in her eyes and spoke to her calmly.

"Karen, I've had plenty of time to think about this and you were right. I was so wrong and I hope you can forgive me..."

Karen cut me off in mid-sentence, "Look, I have to get the kids ready. My mother will be here any minute to pick them up. You can tell me what you have to say after she comes, so uh..."

Karen walked over to the door and opened it. I knew that was my clue to leave. I walked up to the door and stopped and looked at her.

"Can you call me after the kids are gone?" I asked.

Without looking at me, she nodded.

I walked back to my place thinking, *"Damn, she's not going to make this easy..."* I stepped inside my apartment and sat by the phone waiting for it to ring. Thirty minutes had passed and still no ring. She wasn't going to call. That was just her way of getting me out of her apartment. She didn't want to hear anything that I had to say. I got up and headed for the couch and suddenly, the phone rang. "Hello," I said.

"They're gone, what do you want?"

"Can I come over now?" I asked nicely.

"Can't you say what you have to say right now?" she asked.

"Well... How about we go for a ride, maybe get something to eat?"

There was a long pause on the line but I knew she couldn't resist a free meal. She agreed. I walked back outside and Karen had already come down and was waiting by the car. We both climbed in and I pulled out of the parking space then quickly through the parking lot. I asked her what she wanted to eat and she just shrugged her shoulders.

"How about pizza?" I asked.

Still, only a shrug. I pulled into the Wendy's and ordered a couple of burger meals with drinks. I pulled up to the window, paid for the food then pulled up and received the bag and two drinks. I darted out of the driveway and sped off into traffic. While I drove Karen ate. After about thirty minutes later, I pulled onto the dirt road. That's right, I took her to Fingers Reach. After climbing the steep hilly roads, I turned on my parking lights and pulled into an open spot. Finally she spoke, "This is really pretty. I've never been here. How come you've never brought me here before?" she asked.

"I'll bring you here as many times as you want from now on if you let me."

"You hurt me Bobby," she said then chucked a few fries in her mouth.

"I know I did and I'm sorry. I'm sorry for everything. I'm sorry I said that I didn't want the baby and for saying that I didn't love you. I do, and not because of the baby. After thinking about how you are and what we've had, I realized that it is you that I should be with, nobody else. And you're right, I've never been married and I'm truly sorry for lying to you. Please forgive me Karen and say that we can be together; me, you, and the kids."

Karen looked at me. I could see her eyes welling up with tears. My acting was so good that I was misting up myself. She placed her hand on mine then leaned over and gave me a kiss. We kissed and caressed for over an hour. All the cars were gone and she was looking like she wanted to fully make up but all I wanted was the answer that I was seeking. She opened her door and got out of the car then got in the back. I followed, then finally, she broke.

"Do you mean that Bobby? Do you really mean that you will be with me no matter what?" she asked.

"Yes, I really do."

"That's nice to know because yesterday I found out that I'm not pregnant. I don't know why my period was late but it did come, so you can relax," she said smiling.

I wasn't smiling though. I was still hot under my collar. I had gotten all the information that I needed from her conniving ass and was now ready to go back and drop her back home. Instead, I thought, *"What the hell, I have a condom in the glove box. One more as a good bye won't hurt."*

After rocking the car for a while, we climbed back into the front seats and I took Karen back home. I walked her to her door and then told her everything that Fran had told me. I told her that I just needed to hear it from her and that I couldn't ever be with someone who could be as callous as she was. Then I informed her that we were done. Oh and don't worry, at the lake, I wore a condom AND pulled out.

<u>Chapter 18 - The Other Half</u>

Two weeks had passed and I still had no contact with Michelle. I did hear from Donald. He told me that he had spoken with her and had told him that she had gotten the job. She also informed him on her scheduled return to Atlanta to handle her affairs. I had decided to wait until her return before confronting her about Allison and to give her the good news about the baby. I was actually quite taken aback that she had not contacted me. It was killing me this entire time and I'm sure that she knows that I'm hurting.

Another week had passed, still nothing from Michelle. I did however, see Karen a few times over the weeks. She would look at me in such an apologetic and hurt manner that I almost felt sorry for her but I would merely wave hello and continue on. Even though I hadn't been physically relieved in weeks, I wasn't about to get involved with her again. It was starting to look like things were over with Michelle as well but I couldn't give up on her. I'd waited so long for her. "*So what if she likes a little 'Clam dippin,' that's not so bad. I mean, what can they do? I don't know but all I do know is... she likes it. If she likes it that much, maybe all three of us can get together? What am I saying? Hell no, I'm not sharing her with anybody! Whatever Allison can do, I can do and give her the stiffness too,*" I thought.

Another week had passed and I was tired of taking matters into my own hands. Michelle was back and I had to see her. I drove over and dropped in on my parents. Dad of course was what…? Thaaaat's right, you guessed it, sitting on the porch and mom was in the dining room talking to who…? Yep, her sister.

After stopping to talk with my dad, I stepped inside and gave my mother a hug and gestured for her not to get off the phone. I let her know that I was returning shortly. I walked through the kitchen and out the back door. I walked out of the yard and through the alley which lead to the street. As I climbed the walkway toward Michelle's house, I could see them. Michelle was standing in front of her house hugging him. I first thought that it had to be a relative or just a friend. After all, I did jump to that conclusion with her cousin Derric. I decided to give her the benefit of the doubt. Then they kissed. I'm talking about a tongue embracing, lip locking, you're my woman kind of kiss. *"Damn, I'm too late! Now who in the hell is that!?"* I screamed inside my head.

Well of course I couldn't walk up there now. Just as I was about to turn around, she saw me. I paused for a second, looked at my watch then continued on. As I headed in their direction, I could see Michelle's lips move as she whispered something to the man. He looked over as to examine me then back to her. I quickly turned and made my way up the stairs to Donald's mother's house. After reaching the door, I looked back over my shoulder at the couple. They were still looking over at me. I couldn't help it. I then did the only thing that my mind directed, I waved. Neither of them waved back. I didn't expect Donald's mom to answer the door but she was the only option that I had. Suddenly, I heard the rattles at the door. After a brief succession of knobs being turned, the door opened. It was Donald. "What are you doing here?" I asked

"Mom wasn't feeling too well yesterday so I stayed over. What are YOU doing here if you didn't think that I was here?"

"Well I was going to try to talk to Michelle about... well, you know but as I walked up toward her house I saw her and her new guy. I guess that's who he is. I turned into here trying not to look so stupid."

"Well for one thing, you're wrong. That's not her new guy, that's her husband. I met his sorry ass last night. She said that he helped her move the rest of her stuff up."

"But I thought she had a restraining order against him!" I said looking surprised.

"Does he look restrained to you?" Donald said displaying a silly look on his face.

"Well I guess not. Guess that was all just a load of bull," I said shaking my head.

"No, it wasn't all a load of crap. He did say last night that he was moving up here too so they could reconcile their differences and get things back right."

"By the way they were just going at it, I'd say that they've already reconciled their differences," I said depressingly.

"So you're finally gonna give up on her?"

I stood there contemplating for a few seconds then looked down towards the floor, "I guess so."

"Finally! Now you see that I wasn't lying to you. I mean, she's good and all but not the 'throw yourself out of a window' kind of good, damn. I mean, she can do that 'swirly twirly' thing with her tongue and all but..."

I looked up at Donald angrily indicating that he had said enough and he read my signal loud and clear.

I left Donald's after Michelle and her spouse had vacated. I was crushed beyond belief. I had finally saw her for who and what she really was, a liar and a whore. I now knew that everything that everyone had told me about her was true. Fred, my mother, Donald and even Fran, they were all just trying to protect me from her. A part of my mind still didn't want to believe it but I knew. I felt sick. I loved this woman so much for so long but I was nothing to her but a mere toy. She had never planned for us to be together. She still had her husband, Allison and anybody else. I'm pretty sure that Donald was still easing his way over there too, he just didn't want to hurt me any more than I already was. I didn't blame him much, it was free and she could do that swirly tongue thing that he had mentioned. I knew that I had to come to grips with this thing but it was really difficult.

Michelle had truly deceived me, for years. Now I wanted her, like Karen, to tell me the truth. This was the only way I could have complete closure. Although I had no doubt in my mind of who she really was, I needed to hear it from her mouth and hers alone. She owed me that.

Chapter 19 - Revenge

Just over three weeks had passed and I continued conducting my normal routine. I went to work, visited with my parents and waved to Karen upon my return home. It was Friday and just enough time had passed for Michelle to really feel comfortable. She was now settled at home and with her new job. I was in constant contact with Donald throughout the weeks and he kept me updated with her routine. Allison every Thursday night and Steven on Fridays. He said that Steven would pick her up and drop her off every day but on Fridays she would drive herself and he would come over about seven o'clock then they would go out. He also reported that Steven would spend the night every Friday.

Later that evening, I rode over and parked my car in front of my parent's home and walked over to Donald's mom's through the alley. Donald opened the back door as I climbed the stairs. We walked to the front of the house and sat on the couch. We sat talking for over an hour until just as he described, Steven's car pulled up. The large man stepped out of the car and walked up to the door. Not sure if they were going out or staying in, I hesitated. Donald handed me the keys to his black Isuzu and I quickly rose and slithered out the gate. After reaching Donald's vehicle, I quietly unlocked the door and slid inside. I sat still and quiet for about twenty minutes before the couple appeared in my view. Steven had his arm around his wife and escorted her to the car. He opened the door to his lavish brand new Mercedes Sedan; boy I hate him. He then walked around to the driver's side of the vehicle and slid into the plush leather seat. I could hear the car's engine rev up. Seconds later, they pulled off. I started Donald's car and quickly pulled out in pursuit. I waited until they were out of sight before turning on the headlights.

I followed the vehicle through the city and kept plenty of distance as I followed. I suddenly realize that the route that they were taking was so familiar. We were heading in the direction of Fingers Reach. *No way!* I thought. But as sure as I'm telling you this crazy story, they turned onto the dirt road leading to the overlook. I waited until they were far in the distance then pulled into the parking lot of the country store. I sat there for twenty minutes or so before heading up the road.

After reaching the top of the steep incline, I turned off the headlights to the vehicle and rode up the dirt parking area with only the parking lights on. There sitting in our usual spot was his classy automobile. The windows were already half covered with steam. This angered me. *The nerve of this nasty hussy*! I thought. I wasn't sure why I sat there for so long but I had seen enough. I turned on the ignition and tuned on the headlights as I made a "U" turn to head down the hill. I clicked on the "high beam" switch as I turned in his car's direction. I could see his head pop up through the steamed windows. I turned the switch off and headed down the hill and back to Donald's. If I hadn't already felt foolish enough. I'm not even sure why I followed them now.

I returned the keys to Donald. When he asked me what I had seen, I merely replied... "Enough." We sat and talked for about an hour. He tried cheering me up by feeding me more information on some of Michelle's whoring escapades. It didn't help.

"Bobby, you look at this as one of the worse things that could have happened to you, when it's actually one of the best," he said.

"What if you had found out how she really was after you had married her?" he continued.

"I don't know man."

"Hurt! Worse than you do right now, that's for sure."

"You're still doing her too, aren't you?" I asked.

"Huh?"

"You heard me, you've been doing her too, haven't you?" I asked again forcefully.

Donald lowered his head then thought for a second, "Like I said, you know I've never lied to you so yes. Since she's been back, Wednesday has been my night."

"Knowing how I feel about her and that doesn't bother you?" I asked looking hurt.

"I mean, I feel a little bad but then you know... the 'swirly twirly' man. I just can't resist it!"

I picked up my keys and headed for the front door. As I walked through the gate the couple pulled up, both looking in my direction. I headed back down the hill to my car. I didn't go back inside my parent's house. I just got into my car and drove home.

I waited to the following Tuesday before returning. It wasn't Steven's, Allison's, or Donald's night. I waited on the back porch of my parents' for the expensive auto to pull up. At 5:15 it did just that. The Mercedes slowly pulled in front of the house and Michelle made her departure. I trotted down the stairs and out the gate. I stopped at the corner of the alley and waited until Steven had pulled away from the curb. I walked up the hill, through the entranceway and up to the front door. I knocked on the front door while looking around, to ensure that the Mercedes had not returned.

I could hear her advancing toward the door. As the door opened, I could see her look of excitement quickly dissipate after noticing that it wasn't the driver of the Mercedes.

"What are you doing here?" she asked.

"I needed to see you. I was at my mom's and saw your car, thought I would stop to see if you were here."

"Well, I'm here, what do you want?"

"What I've always wanted... you."

"You're having a kid, aren't you? You need to be a good father," she said sarcastically.

"That's what I've been wanting to talk to you about. She's not pregnant. She was just trying to keep me from being with you and I guess her plan worked."

I knew by saying something like that to her, she would have to prove Karen wrong. That's one thing that I knew about Michelle, she was very competitive.

"She knew that you wouldn't stand by me through something like that so she wanted to prove it to me," I continued.

Michelle opened the door and stepped back leaving me room to enter. I noticed how she slyly looked up the street just to make sure that Steven was truly gone.

"It wasn't because she was pregnant that I got angry, it was because you withheld it from me," she said.

"Well now that it's not true, are you going to continue to make me suffer or have you already found someone else?"

"No silly, there's no one else. I've missed you so much."

"I've missed you too and I'm glad that it all worked out."

I knew that it was all just a game to her but the fool in me still wanted to believe the tramp.

I walked up to her and we kissed. We kissed long and passionately. We walked over to the couch and began our sexual festival. I could only image Donald peering through his binoculars at us. I didn't care, I wanted him to know that Tuesday's would be mine and that he could have what was left on Wednesday. Before it was all said and done, I sat up on the couch to enjoy the pleasures of the "swirly twirly." We talked for a while afterwards about what had transpired during our absence from one another, which were all lies. Then it hit me, Friday was her date night with Steven.

"Hey, let's get a blanket and do what we said we were going to do at Fingers Reach," I said while looking at her in a seductive manner.

I knew the slut wouldn't be able to resist something as freaky as that. I also knew that she had to consider what Steven would think.

"Friday?" she asked.

"Yeah, I'll meet you there straight from work. I'll bring a bottle of wine and we can sip and talk 'til everyone leaves. It'll be fun."

I could see her mind spinning, contemplating what and how to do it. I reached over and fondled her then kissed her neck.

"Ok," she whispered.

"Six o'clock?" I asked.

"Ok, that sounds good," she replied smiling.

I kissed her again then made my exit. I was smiling all the way home. I had made up my mind that I was going to get her tipsy first then hit her with everything. I was going to tell her how I saw her and Allison and listen to her deny it. Then I was going to ask her about Steven and wait for her to lie and tell her how I watched them in the exact same spot that we were sitting in. How Fred told me everything that happened in junior high school and in high school. And definitely what Donald had told me about the two of them. I knew that she would only get pissed off and ask me to take her home but somehow, I knew that it would make me feel whole again.

The next morning, I got up and got dressed for work. I had overslept and was in bit of a rush. My phone rang but I didn't answer. I had to go. I snatched my keys from the table and rushed out the door and down the stairs onto the stoop. As I headed down the steps it was then that I noticed the large figure leaning against my car. It was Steven. Since we had never met formerly I pretended not to know who he was.

"Excuse me man, is there something that I can do for you?" I asked.

He raised himself off of my car and stepped toward me.

"Yes sir, there is. You can stay the hell away from my wife is what you can do," he said bitterly.

He was a lot bigger than he looked from a distance and since my knife was in the glove box of my car I thought I'd better act a little sensible in this situation. I revved back and placed both of my hands in front of my chest as if to keep him at bay.

"Look man, I was told by her that you two are no longer together," I said.

"Well we are."

"Maybe you're the only one that knows that."

"If I see you hanging around her house again, I'm telling you, there's going to be a problem."

"If she tells me not to come there then I won't. I'll wait for her call," I said sarcastically.

He turned and walked back over to his car that was parked on the opposite side of the parking lot. He quickly climbed in and sped off. I figured only two things could have happened last night. One: he did in fact double back to see if she was doing something or somebody else or two: it was Donald. That's right, Donald had probably seen Michelle and I together. He probably had gotten jealous and informed Steven. He did say that he had met him and got all chummy with him, who knows. Either way, Steven knew more than I expected.

Friday came quickly. I never received a call from Michelle asking me to leave her alone. I called her house and she quickly answered.

"Hey Baby!" she answered.

"Hello sexy, are we still on for this evening?" I asked.

"We sure are. You want me to pick something up to eat on my way? You know you're going to need all of your strength," she said chuckling.

"Sure, anything you want, you decide."

"Alright, I should be there by 6:30 then."

"Ok, I can't wait."

"Me either. See you soon baby, bye."

We ended the call and I chuckled to myself. *"What a fake,"* I thought.

The flashing lights illuminated the entire parking area. I could see the detectives examining her motionless body from the backseat of the squad car. The handcuffs were cutting through my wrists and my clothing was soiled from them holding me down on the ground. I watched on as they measured my foot prints in the dirt and dusted her car for prints. I sat there for over an hour before being transported to the police station. There, I was interrogated for hours. I was able to make a phone call so I telephoned my dad. I told him that I was being charged with murder and he said that he would contact a lawyer. I had seen enough television to know that it was time to stay quiet. I was taken to be photographed then fingerprinted. It was if I was in a deep fog.

When the lawyer finally arrived, I was directed to a room where he was already sitting. His name was Thomas Bland. His father and mine were very close friends. They had served in the Army together years ago. I had never met Thomas but had met his father at the house several times. Of course, his first question was, "What happened?" I sat back in the cold metal seat and told him everything.

"I headed up to Fingers Reach. Traffic was pretty congested when I left work. I was supposed to meet Michelle there at 6:30. I arrived around seven o'clock because of the traffic backup. I thought she would have already left or was going to be pissed because she would have been waiting for about a half hour. But I drove up the hill and saw her parked car. I could see her sitting there. I pulled up beside her and got out of the car. I walked over and could hear the radio playing due to the window being down. I leaned over to give her a kiss and could see the blood running down her chest saturating her blouse. I called out to her over and over but she didn't move. I jumped in my car and called the police from the pay phone at the 7-11 and drove back here. The next thing I know sirens are blaring up the hill and I'm being slammed to the ground and handcuffed."

"Did the officers read you your Miranda rights?" he asked.

"Yes."

"When they were interrogating you, what did you tell them?"

"I kept telling them that I didn't do it."

"How did you get the blood on your shirt and hands?"

"I guess when I leaned over to get her phone, it got on my shirt; I'm not sure. When I first saw the blood, I thought she could still be alive so I tried to put pressure on the cut to stop the bleeding. It was so much blood," I whimpered trying to keep my composure.

"Ok, I don't want you to worry, I'm going to find out what kind of evidence that they have and see about getting you out of here. You'll probably have to stay in here until Monday but that's about it hopefully."

Well as you might have already guessed, that Monday came and the next Monday and many after that. I was not released. It seems that there were no other fingerprints at the scene or in her car but mine. No footprints other than mine were near or around the car. I had motive. I was jealous of Steven. I found out that she was screwing around with a woman and several people that they interviewed from the old neighborhood stated that I was obsessed with her, including Donald. Fran had stated that I told her that I was going to kill Michelle. I'm not quite sure why but you never know with Fran.

I'll never forget that autumn morning when I was escorted to the room where Thomas stood. "How are you holding up?" he asked.

"I'm making it," I responded.

"They want to offer you a deal," he said while unbuttoning his suit jacket.

"A deal?"

"Yes, the D.A. is offering fifteen years and murder in the second, you could be out in eight."

"Fifteen years?!"

"Look, every shred of evidence points to you, every bit. The maximum sentence for murder is life here, without the possibility of parole. It's a good deal."

"I shouldn't have to do one day. I didn't do this. What about the truth?"

"It's not about the truth Bobby, it's what we can prove."

Those words will live in my head until my last breath. I was about to do hard time for a crime that I didn't commit. Thomas told me that I only had until the next morning to give them an answer and if we went to trial, they were going for the maximum punishment. Can you imagine how many people are currently incarcerated for a crime that they didn't commit? Ninety to ninety-five percent of federal and local cases have resulted in plea bargains. You can only imagine how many were innocent. Deals are made as if we are just pieces on a chest board. I too added to that percentage as my attorney instructed. He said that the odds of us winning the case wasn't favorable and if found guilty, I could very easily spend the rest of my life in prison. What would you do?

After accepting the deal, I was shipped off to the Brockbridge Correctional Facility in Jessup Maryland. I was angry. Angry at my attorney, Donald, Fran, and everybody else that helped put me away. It wasn't right. It was a hard transformation for me. One that I couldn't and didn't want to ever get used to. I was away from everybody that I cared about or who cared about me. My parents would visit pretty often but I didn't want them to see like this, not in here caged up like an animal.

Chapter 20 - All for Love

I had now been incarcerated for almost three years before I was to learn who actually murdered her. I was notified that I was to have a visitor. After being escorted to the visitor's area and seated, I sat awaiting my parents to enter the room. My jaw dropped when in walked the last person that I would have expected. I sat there motionless, not knowing what to expect. I lowered my head in somewhat shame as I listened to the seat across from me being pulled out.

"How are you doing?" I was quickly asked.

"I'm hangin' in there," I replied masking my true feeling.

"I wanted to come sooner but I didn't know if I should."

"Why shouldn't you?" I asked.

"I know how it is in here. You go through a lot, mostly in your head."

"Yeah, and how would you know that?"

"Because I've been inside before. Actually, for something similar to what you're in here for now."

"I didn't know that. So you were in for doing nothing too," I said while letting out a fake laugh.

"No... I was actually guilty."

"Well I'm not," I said then slouched back in the chair.

"I know."

"You know? How can you be so sure?"

At that very moment, I knew. I knew why I was having this visit and I now knew who killed Michelle.

"You didn't think for one minute that I was going to let that tramp treat you like that did you?"

"But I..." I couldn't get my sentence out before I was interrupted.

"But you were weak! She led you around like a little puppy and I grew tired of it. I wasn't about to let her treat my Bobby like that. Oh yes, I've had an eye on you. Now I did like the other girl though. You know, the one with the kids. She seemed to genuinely care for you. But that other thing, I knew she was bad news. I know it's hard in here and if you want, you can tell them what I did and I'll do the rest of the time for you but I don't think you'd do that. I know how much you love me."

I said nothing. I sat there taking it all in. When the visiting time was over, I rose from my seat and headed for the door while being escorted by the guard. After reaching the door, I looked back and said it. "I love you, Sandra."

She was right, I would never give her up. Sandra loved me and I adored her. She was like a mother, big sister and of course, my sex instructor the entire time she lived with us. I hated to see her leave and only heard from her on my birthdays and an occasional Christmas. But she had never left the area.

I did eight of my fifteen years. The day I walked out I was met by my now current wife, Karen. I contacted her the day after Sandra visited me and she wrote to me every day and visited me at least once a month. She truly loved me. And oh yeah, we now have an eight month old son, Bobby Junior.